Mystery Horse

Mystery Horse

by MARGARET GOFF CLARK

SCHOLASTIC BOOK SERVICES
NEW YORK • TORONTO • LONDON • AUCKLAND • SYDNEY • TOKYO

To Sherry, with love

Copyright © 1972 by Margaret Goff Clark. This edition is published by Scholastic Book Services, a division of Scholastic Magazines, Inc., by arrangement with Dodd, Mead and Company.

1st printing .... December 1973

Printed in the U.S.A.

The author wishes to thank her Tuscarora friends for their information, kindness, and help.

RIDGE ROAD

BORDER OF RESERVATION

KIENUKA
YOUNG ORCHARD

CLEARING

TUSCARORA RESERVATION

CORN

RIDING TRAILS

HARVEY STABLES

PRACT

TO NIAGARA FALLS

UPPER MOUNTAIN ROAD

WALMORE ROAD
TO PICNIC GROUNDS

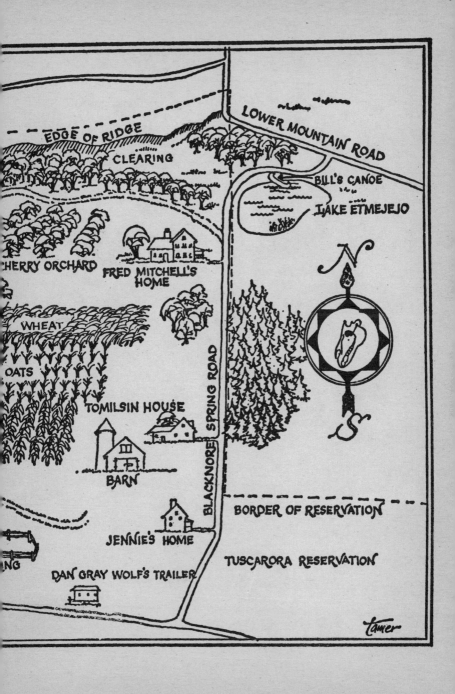

CHAPTER
1

Jennie Longboat ran down the steps from the porch and scanned the dark lawn.

Where *was* Miranda? It wasn't like her to go out alone at night, especially on such a black night as this. Although she was fourteen, only a year younger than Jennie, she seemed half afraid of the dark.

"I'm used to the bright lights," she had said. Until a month ago when Miranda came here to board with Jennie and her grandparents at the Tuscarora Indian Reservation, she had lived in the city of Buffalo, thirty miles away.

"You're safer here on the reservation than you'd be in the city," Jennie reassured her then, but Miranda had only shuddered.

Now here it was, almost eleven o'clock, and Miranda Young was not in the house. Jennie's grandparents were in bed and Jennie had gone up to her room, expecting to find Miranda there. The room was empty. Not wanting to alarm her grandmother, Jennie had quietly searched the house, and then, flashlight in hand, had gone outdoors.

Probably it was foolish to be worried, but there was no place for a girl to go on the Tuscarora Reservation, not unless she had a car. Except for the Tomilsin house, one hundred yards to the north, only fields and woods bordered the Blacknose Spring Road for half a mile in either direction. The nearest city, Niagara Falls, was more than five miles away.

As Jennie circled the house, she beamed her flashlight across the dark lawn and then turned it onto the low bushes that edged the front porch.

Nothing moved, and all was silent except for the *chunk* of frogs in the roadside ditch and the occasional *whoosh* of a car in the distance.

She paused, aware of something strange and eerie about this night. Not a star shone and the air felt heavy. A wisp of vapor floated past a few feet above the ground. Jennie backed nervously away. She had a fleeting impression that some danger lurked nearby, like a beast ready to pounce.

I'm being silly, she told herself firmly. The dinner conversation that night must have put ideas into her head. Grandma had told Miranda about the old Tuscarora legend of the Flying Heads and had gone on and on with stories of those strange, bodiless witches that flew through the air. Their long hair flamed like fire and they had a reputation for devouring people.

Jennie had heard them before, of course. But it was the way Miranda listened, round-eyed, that made the tales seem frightening to Jennie, too. Miranda wasn't an Indian, so the tales were new to her, and Grandma, who enjoyed having a fresh audience, had told them extra vividly.

Jennie shrugged off her moment of uneasiness. What nonsense to be afraid in her own backyard! She often walked down the road to Uncle Fred's at night or just stood in the yard inhaling the cool, damp scent of darkness. There was a beauty and mystery about night that intrigued her, and often when she stared up at the stars she felt as if she were on the threshold of a more exciting life than she had ever known. Why, then, should she be uneasy tonight?

Just as she had told Miranda, the Tuscarora Indian Reservation was one of the safest places in the world. One of the dullest, too, she thought gloomily. She had lived here all her life and the world outside looked like the promised land.

It was hard for Jennie to understand why Miranda thought it was such fun to board with her and her grandparents. Although Jennie loved her home, she was sure it must seem small and plain to a city girl. Grandpa Mitchell had built the house himself, little by little, as he had been able to buy the materials. Bankers wouldn't lend him money for a house because they couldn't take over reservation land belonging to an Indian if he failed to keep up his mortgage payments.

Jennie glanced toward the barn, set back in the field halfway between her home and the Tomilsin house. Perhaps Miranda was there. She often went out during the day to see the horses. But no light showed through the small windows of the barn.

When she shifted her gaze to the Tomilsin house, she found it, too, was completely dark. That left only Uncle Fred's, half a mile down the road. Miranda liked Fred Mitchell and his family, so it was just possible she might have gone there.

Jennie hesitated. She could phone her uncle, but that might awaken Grandma or Grandpa. Little as she liked the idea of walking to Uncle Fred's tonight, she would have to do it. She couldn't sleep till she found Miranda.

With a last glance at the house, she cut across the grass and started down the dark road. If she didn't find Miranda there, at least Uncle Fred would know what to do next.

Usually Jennie felt she understood Miranda, but for the past few days the other girl had seemed like a stranger. Today she had been silent and wrapped in her own thoughts. In the middle of the afternoon she had gone out without telling anyone where she was going and had not returned until Jennie and her grandparents were at the dinner table.

Jennie realized how little she really knew about Miranda. She had never even seen her until a month ago when Miranda's aunt had come to the door looking for a place where her orphaned niece could spend the summer. She was an English teacher in a Buffalo college and she had a chance to take a tour of the British Isles, she explained. She wanted a good summer home in the country for Miranda. One of the aunt's fellow teachers, Miss Hugo, had been studying Tuscarora legends and history for a thesis, and suggested that the Mitchells might be willing to board Miranda with them on the reservation. Miss Hugo had come to know and like them while gathering information for her thesis.

Jennie had listened hopefully while Miranda's aunt talked with Grandma. Few non-Indians lived on the reservation, but, thought Jennie, there was no reason why one white girl couldn't stay with an Indian family. Miss Hugo had boarded on the reservation last summer. Jennie had often longed to have a girl her own age in the house and she was sorry when she heard her grandmother explain that they had no extra bedroom.

Miranda had appeared disappointed, too. To Jennie's sympathetic eyes, the pretty blonde girl had the thin, forlorn look of an abandoned kitten.

"She can share my room," Jennie had offered warmly. "I can get the cot from the attic for me."

And that had settled it.

They had gotten along well from the very start and shared confidences as well as a room. Jennie admitted her secret liking for the neighbor boy, Bill Tomilsin. Miranda told Jennie how much she still missed her

mother and stepfather who had been killed in an auto-
mobile accident a little over a year before. She said she
didn't think she could have lived through those first
terrible days if it hadn't been for the kindness of Gary,
her stepbrother. She had scarcely known him until then,
for he had lived away from home ever since his father
had remarried. For that matter, she rarely saw him now,
but he had helped her when she needed him.

It seemed to Jennie that she and Miranda had been
friends for years. Something must have upset her to
make her disappear like this. Or something had happened
to her . . . .

Jennie rushed on, though mosquitoes buzzed around
her head and the moist heat made her thick black hair
cling to her neck. Surely a storm must be coming.

She had reached a lonely section of the road where
a grove of pine trees stood on her right, and on her left
was a dense growth of maple, oak, and beech. She could
smell the pines, but she couldn't see them. The night
was so dark the world seemed to end at the edge of the
road.

Suddenly, to her dismay, she heard running footsteps
behind her. Her heart beat faster and she swung around,
trying to see who was approaching.

CHAPTER

2

Jennie called out nervously, "Who is it?"

"Just a couple of Indians," was the amused reply.

"Oh, Bill!" A tall, broad-shouldered boy loomed up beside her. She might have known it would be Bill Tomilsin. He ran up the road almost every night — though not this late — keeping in shape for lacrosse and basketball.

Close behind him came another shorter and heavier young man. Jennie recognized Dan Gray Wolf, a Sioux from North Dakota, a college student who was spending the summer in a trailer on the Upper Mountain Road.

The two boys slowed to a walk and Dan said in his solemn, unsmiling way, "Hello, Jennie Longboat."

Bill asked, "Where are you headed this time of night?"

"I'm looking for Miranda. She's not in the house and

I don't know where she is."

Bill said calmly, "She's old enough to look after herself."

"I know it." Jennie felt foolish. "But just the same I'm worried about her. I'm going to see if she's at Uncle Fred's."

"We're going past there. I want to check on my canoe at the pond," Bill told her. "Dan saw Pete Campbell paddling around in a boat like mine this afternoon. You know who I mean, that red-haired fellow who helps out at the riding stables."

Jennie nodded. "I couldn't miss that hair."

Dan was jogging a few paces ahead of them but Bill walked companionably beside Jennie. She was surprised and pleased. Since he was almost two years older than she, she had long ago given up hope that he would pay any attention to her. His conversation was generally limited to a friendly "Hi!" as he dashed past on his way to basketball practice or his various after-school jobs.

Bill continued to grumble about Pete Campbell. "I never told him he could take my canoe and this isn't the first time he's used it. I wouldn't mind, but he never puts it back where it belongs. There's a storm coming, sure, and I bet he left it half in the water where it can blow out in the pond and maybe turn over."

Jennie knew the pond he referred to was little Lake Etmejejo, located at the end of the Blacknose Spring Road.

"It feels like a storm," she agreed. "It's a weird night.

I don't see why Miranda would go out alone on a night like this."

Dan Gray Wolf came back toward them. "Every time I see Miranda she's in the barn, talking to Fair Lady," he commented.

"The barn's dark," said Jennie. "I didn't look there."

"Never saw any horse take to a person as fast as Fair Lady took to Miranda," put in Bill.

Dan jogged a circle around the other two. "I'm going on home, Bill, long as you have company."

"OK," Bill agreed. "Come over tomorrow after work."

"Right. So long, Jennie." Dan stopped jogging for a final word. "If I see Miranda I'll tell her you're looking for her."

Jennie was pleased at his thoughtfulness. "Thanks so much."

Dan still lingered, staring at Jennie through the darkness. "Where'd you get that name, Longboat?" he asked. "That's a real Indian name."

Jennie smiled. "Like Gray Wolf?"

"Yeah. You hear a name like Longboat or Gray Wolf or Running Bear and you know it belongs to an Indian. Most of you Tuscaroras have white man's names."

"Most of our ancestors intermarried with the whites," said Jennie. "But I don't believe the Longboats did, at least, not much."

"Guess not. You look like an Indian," commented Dan. His tone was warmly approving. "I'm not used to a reservation like this where the houses look like ordinary farmhouses and I can't tell if I'm on Indian land or off it. It's a treat to see a real Indian face." He lifted his hand. "See you."

Dan's square-set form was swallowed by the gloom.

"Congratulations," said Bill. "Whether you know it or not, Dan just paid you a big compliment." After a pause he added, "And I agree with him."

Jennie murmured, "Thank you." His praise made her so happy she had a floating sensation, as if her body were weightless. She wanted to tell him that she liked the way he looked, too, but before she could find the words, he turned to another subject.

"Speaking of Fair Lady," he said, "that filly is going to buy me a car so I can get back and forth to school in Buffalo this fall. Mr. Trent's particular how I look after her, but he pays well. Did I ever tell you how I got the job of keeping her?"

"No, you didn't." He had rarely told her anything, thought Jennie.

"Well, this fellow, Gordon Trent, came along one day about two weeks ago. Lives near Buffalo. He said he asked about boarding Fair Lady at Harvey's Riding Stables. They said they were full up—everybody's riding lately—but to ask me because I might let her share the barn with my horse. Of course I said sure. Old Cloud's never had such high-class company. Fair Lady comes from fine Arabian stock, you know."

Jennie had never exchanged more than a few words

with Gordon Trent, the owner of Fair Lady, but each time he drove up to the barn in his little green Porsche convertible, he seemed like a visitor from what she thought of as the world outside—a world of laughing young men and women who rode in open cars with their hair blowing.

"Is Mr. Trent in college?" she asked.

"No. He's too old. He must be almost thirty. Well, I suppose he could be in college, anyway, but he isn't. He has a job selling life insurance."

The sudden blast of a train whistle made Jennie gasp.

Bill chuckled. "That's a diesel at the Walmore Road crossing."

"That's more than three miles away! It sounded as if it were right behind us."

"It's the weather," said Bill. "Sounds travel faster on a hot, humid night like this."

"You talk like my science teacher."

"My favorite subject. I like all kinds of science. In fact, I'm going to be a doctor if I can swing it."

"Sure," said Jennie. "You're a Bear. You ought to be a good doctor."

"You and your legends," Bill said teasingly. "I know that one, too, about the old woman from the Bear Clan. She took care of the friend of some good spirit when he was sick and he taught her how to use herbs to cure all kinds of diseases."

"The good spirit was Tarenyawagon," Jennie informed him. She had an impulse to tell Bill about her own desire to go to college to study music and how set her grandmother was against it, but since it was a family matter she knew she couldn't discuss it with a neighbor.

"Listen!" Bill exclaimed. "What's that?"

He and Jennie stopped and looked back. No one was in sight, but Jennie could hear someone hurrying down the road after them.

A voice called out, "Hel-loo!"

Jennie beamed her flashlight in the direction of the voice. It illuminated a short, slender girl in pink slacks and sandals. Jennie felt a rush of relief. "It's Miranda!"

Miranda caught up with them. "Why—didn't you— tell me you were going out?" she demanded breathlessly. Her long blonde hair was tangled and her face was flushed. "I saw Dan go by the house and he told me where you were."

"I came out to look for you!" Jennie said indignantly. "Where were you?"

"Right on the porch. I fell asleep on the glider."

"On the glider!" Jennie looked at Miranda in amazement. "I didn't see you there!"

Bill laughed. "See? I told you there was no reason to worry."

Jennie was baffled. How had she missed seeing Miranda on the glider? True, she hadn't gone over to it, but wouldn't she have noticed if someone had been sleeping there?

Miranda's explanation didn't ring true for still another reason. The pink slacks, which had been clean and whole at dinner, were now muddy at the knees and had a long rip in the left leg. Several burrs were caught in the fabric near the ankles. Miranda had been someplace besides on the porch and the road. But why was she lying about it?

CHAPTER

3

Jennie stared at Miranda in disbelief. Yet, she did not argue with her. Grandma said it was impolite to doubt the word of a friend or guest. Sarah Mitchell had strict ideas concerning the way an Indian should act, and Jennie had a great deal of respect for the code which had been passed down by word of mouth from one Tuscarora to another for centuries. As Grandma said, if everyone lived by the Indian traditions, it would be a better world.

Miranda broke the awkward silence. "Where were you going?"

"To Uncle Fred's to look for you," answered Jennie. "And Bill was headed for Lake Etmejejo to look for his canoe."

"It isn't far to the lake," said Bill. "Why don't you go with me; then I can walk you home."

To Jennie's surprise, Miranda objected. "I think we ought to go home now. It's going to rain."

"That's why Bill wants to find his canoe, to be sure it's safe," Jennie replied.

Bill looked up at the dark sky. "Do what you want to. I think we have plenty of time before the storm. I'm going on, anyway."

"*I* say we should go back!" declared Miranda. "Come on, Bill!"

Again Jennie was puzzled. Why was Miranda so insistent? Jennie, herself, was in no mood to go home for she was enjoying the walk with Bill. It *was* late, though. Probably Miranda was right. Jennie was sure Grandma and Grandpa were alseep, but if they awakened and found that she and Miranda weren't in bed they'd worry.

"If you really want to, we'll go home," Jennie said reluctantly. "Bill doesn't have to go back. Here, Bill, take my flashlight. You'll need it worse than we do."

He refused to take the light. "I can get along."

Miranda said in a voice sharp with impatience, "Well, if he won't come back, we'll go with him. Let's hurry!" She darted ahead, leading the way down the road.

Jennie laughed and followed her. Miranda was as changeable as the wind, and it was no use trying to figure her out.

Miranda kept the lead, and Bill followed with Jennie.

"So now you don't have to stop at your Uncle Fred's," he remarked. "Say, I hear you're helping him with his Tuscarora reading book."

"Oh, mostly I just type what he tells me. He says he

can talk better than he can write. You know what a good storyteller he is. He's putting in sports stories and Indian history, and old legends and he even has jokes. The kids will love to learn Tuscarora from his book."

"You must know Tuscarora pretty well to be able to write it."

"Why not?" said Jennie. "I was brought up on it."

Miranda turned her head to remark plaintively, "When Jennie and her grandmother start talking Indian I can't understand a thing they say." In the gloom and mist her slight, hurrying form reminded Jennie of a sprite from *Midsummer Night's Dream*.

Bill kicked at a stone in the road. "Wish I could talk Tuscarora. My little cousin is learning it in third grade. We didn't study it when I was in the lower grades." He sighed. "My father always says, 'Forget the old ways. We have to live in the world today.' But I don't agree with him any more. I'm an Indian, and I don't want to forget it."

"What made you change?" asked Jennie.

"It's been coming on, but Dan Gray Wolf brought it all into focus. You ought to hear him when he really gets going. He says a lot of his college friends get together and try to figure out how to keep the Indian ways. You know, live close to nature. Get away from all this chasing after money and living like sardines in apartment houses the way some Indians do when they go to the city to work. Indians don't fit in that kind of set up."

Jennie protested. "I think it would [ ] a city. There's more to *do*."

"If it's so great how come all the city [ ] the lakes and mountains the minute they [ ] demanded Bill.

Miranda whirled around. "Jennie wants to get away from the reservation. She wants to be a famous musician." Jennie was startled at the hint of malice in Miranda's voice.

Bill answered quickly, "Why not? Jennie's better than a lot of piano players I hear on TV. Yeah, and she's good on the guitar and clarinet, too."

"I know it," said Miranda. Once more her tone was gentle. "I love it when she practices. You ought to hear her play 'Greensleeves' on the guitar."

Jennie felt embarrassed. "I don't want to be famous. I just want to go to school and study music so I can teach it."

"Nothing wrong with that," Bill said heartily.

"Except her grandma won't let her go," said Miranda. "Mrs. Mitchell says an Indian girl should stay on the reservation and marry a nice Indian boy and have children. She says Jennie has to take a business course and get a job near home." She leaned forward to peer through the darkness at Jennie. "Why do you let your grandmother tell you what to do?"

"Let's not talk about it," said Jennie. She knew it was no use trying to make a white girl like Miranda understand. Grandma was the clan mother of the Beaver Clan

...d that meant she was a very respected person. Besides, she deserved respect because of her age. Jennie couldn't argue with her, ever.

Bill's voice was sympathetic. "How about your grandfather? Would he put in a word for you?"

Silently, Jennie shook her head.

Bill persisted. "Your Uncle Fred, then? He'd help you."

At the mention of her uncle's name, Jennie forgot her reticence. Uncle Fred had been her friend and ally all her life. "Maybe he would help!" she exclaimed. "I should have thought of him. Thanks!"

Bill peered ahead at the lights of Fred Mitchell's house, faintly visible through the trees. "I hear the new chief has been picked," he said.

Jennie looked across at him in surprise. Only the women of the Beaver Clan should know the name of the man they had chosen for the next chief. She, herself, was a Beaver, and, though she was not old enough to vote in the women's council, her grandmother had let her go to the meeting to listen and learn. How happy she had been to hear her uncle's name proposed. Her voice was sharp as she asked Bill, "How do you know?"

"I have ears." In spite of the dark, Jennie could tell he was smiling as he spoke. "And they pick up news here and there."

Miranda squealed, "You mean Jennie's Uncle Fred is going to be a chief?"

Jennie lost her usual self-control. "Don't say that!" she cried.

"Well, it's true, isn't it?" asked Miranda.

"Bill, you ought to know better!" exclaimed Jennie.

Miranda looked from one to the other. "What's the matter?"

"No one's supposed to mention the name of a chief until he's condoled," Jennie explained.

"Condoled?" asked Miranda.

"Installed," said Bill. "We have a ceremony to condole a new chief. It's been done the same way for generations. Isn't that right, Jennie?"

"Yes," she said abruptly.

"Jennie, I won't say his name," Bill went on. "But I want to tell you I think the women picked the right man. I used to think he was too old-fashioned, but he's OK. He was always great to me and the other kids. Took us fishing and stuff like that. He'll be a good chief."

"Bill, please—" began Jennie. Grandma would be horrified at their conversation. Why, Uncle Fred's name hadn't even been passed on by the chiefs' council yet.

Bill would not give up. "Don't tell me you think it's bad luck to even talk about the new chief!"

"Bad luck has nothing to do with it!" she said indignantly. "It isn't right, that's all." But she knew she believed in omens more than she cared to admit. How could she help it, being brought up by a grandmother who kept talking about the old days and the old beliefs?

"Your family's modern," she said. "I guess you don't know much about Indian ways."

"You're right," admitted Bill. "Not talking about a new chief—that's one of the old ways, I suppose. Probably there's some good reason for it, too."

Miranda was impatient. "Will you two stop talking and hurry up!"

"What's the rush?" asked Bill good-humoredly.

"It's late! And I want to get to bed!"

"All right, come on!" Bill lengthened his stride and for a few moments all three walked in silence.

This section of the Blacknose Spring Road followed the eastern border of the Tuscarora Reservation. On the left was Indian land, while the fields to the right belonged to their white neighbors.

As they passed the Mitchell home, Jennie noticed that the porch light was on and the garage was open and empty.

"Uncle Fred's car is out," she remarked. "He must be working overtime tonight." As a shift worker at a Niagara Falls chemical plant, his hours were constantly changing.

Two hundred yards past the Mitchell house was a narrow dirt lane that led to the west through orchards where Jennie and other young Tuscaroras picked cherries every summer. Just beyond the entrance to the lane the main road swung to the right and sloped downhill. Below and on the right, Jennie could see the glimmer of

Lake Etmejejo. Streaks of mist like white veils hung in the air between her and the surface of the water.

"I keep my canoe over on the north side of the lake," Bill said. "Under those willows that hang to the ground."

The three started down the hill. In the silence Jennie could hear the light shuffle of their rubber-soled shoes on the pavement and the hum of a car on the road at the foot of the hill. Her eyes, accustomed to the darkness, picked out the looming shadow of oak trees and the lower, lacy pattern of mountain ash that grew near the road. A damp, fishy smell rose from the lake.

Halfway down the hill, Bill took Jennie's flashlight. "Here's the path. You want to wait here?"

"Of course not," said Miranda. "We'll go with you."

The path led across an open stretch of grass and weeds to the tall willows that bordered the lake. When they reached the shore, Bill pushed aside the branches and shone the flashlight this way and that.

Jennie was the first to see the small red canoe floating a few feet from the beach. "There it is!" She pointed it out to Bill.

"Doggone that Pete Campbell!" he exclaimed. "Good thing I came down here. If we had a storm it could get wrecked." He kicked off his shoes and rolled up his pants. "I'll have to go after it."

The water was not deep, but weeds and silt edged the pond. Jennie could hear the sucking sound of the mud pulling at his feet as Bill came out dragging the canoe behind him. While she held the light, he expertly flipped the boat upside down and shoved it under the sheltering branches of a willow.

"I'm going to give Pete a piece of my mind tomorrow," he commented as he wiped his feet on the grass and put on his sneakers.

"Hurry up!" urged Miranda. "The mosquitoes—"

Bill interrupted. "Listen!"

In the stillness Jennie could hear the hum of a car on the Lower Mountain Road a few hundred yards below them, to the north. Then she heard another sound—a sound that seemed alien to the night—the noise of hoofbeats and the shrill whinny of a horse at the top of the hill where they had been only minutes before.

Coming from the darkness across the lake the clamor was unexpected and startling. As they listened the hoofs continued to clop rapidly and the whinny grew wilder and more frantic.

"Sounds like it's near your Uncle Fred's place," said Bill, his voice softer than usual.

Even as he spoke, the neighing became louder, the hoofbeats drew closer and closer. It seemed as if at any moment horse and rider would appear on the water in front of them. The horse must be on the road—or the lane—thought Jennie, though the sound came from the lake directly in front of them. Puzzled, she moved closer to the water for a better view. From there she could see the lights of her uncle's house at the top of the hill across the lake.

The whinnying noise had reached such a pitch it

seemed to surround her, and the thunder of the hoofs shook the ground. Jennie clapped her hands to her ears and stood, unable to move, staring at the misty lake.

Then, abruptly, there was silence.

Jennie dropped her hands from her ears. Nothing stirred on the lake or along the shore. Where *was* that horse? It must be nearby. She glanced at the road, but that, too, was still empty.

The stories her grandmother had told that very night of the Flying Heads came to her mind. But the Flying Heads were not horses.

Bill let out his breath with an explosive, "Man! What was that?"

Jennie had been so hypnotized by the sound of the horse she had forgotten Bill was there.

"I'm—not sure," she whispered.

Miranda spoke from close behind them. "It was a horse," she said excitedly. "Up in the air. Didn't you see it?"

"A flying horse?" said Bill with a hint of amusement in his voice.

"It was right over the lake." Miranda pointed a shaking finger toward the dark water.

Jennie objected. "I was looking at the lake, but I didn't see anything."

"You didn't look high enough," Miranda said. "It was way up, above the mist."

Bill laughed. "Sure. It had wings. Must have been Pegasus, that horse the Greeks used to write about."

"No," said Miranda. "It didn't have wings. It had a big head, but its body was just bones. A skeleton. I never saw anything so weird in my life."

In spite of herself, Jennie shuddered. Miranda sounded absolutely sure of herself. And the sound *had* come from the air over the lake.

CHAPTER
4

Jennie drew a deep breath. "Let's go home."

As they started up the hill away from the lake, a rush of wind swooped from the north. It buffeted them, blowing their clothes flat against their backs and hurrying them along.

Bill said something Jennie couldn't hear, because the wind carried his words away.

"What?" she shouted.

Bill came closer. "Who'd be out riding at night? On a dark night like this?"

"I *told* you!" cried Miranda. "It wasn't a real horse, and no one was riding it."

"You've had your joke." Bill sounded annoyed.

"It isn't a joke! I told you what I saw!"

There was a lull in the wind, and in the sudden stillness Miranda's voice was too loud.

Jennie turned on her flashlight and beamed it toward the shoulder of the road on one side and then the other.

"The hoofbeats sounded so close. The horse must have been near us. I thought it was going to be on top of us any minute."

"It went right over our heads," Miranda declared.

Bill paid no attention to this remark. "Maybe it was a horse on the Lower Mountain Road."

"No, I'm sure it came from the other direction," Jennie pointed out.

Bill agreed gloomily. "You're right. It seemed to start near your uncle's place."

"I was looking toward his house and I didn't see any horse," said Jennie.

All the way up the hill she looked for hoofprints in the dust at the margins of the road but found none, and her flashlight was beginning to fail.

When they reached the top of the hill, near the lane, Bill paused. "I think I have the answer. You know how sound carries tonight?"

"Yes," agreed Jennie. "We heard that diesel at the Walmore Road and it seemed to be just a few feet away."

"Right. And when we heard the horse we were directly across the lake from here. Sound carries over water better than it does across land. So if a horse came down this lane, we'd hear it plain as anything." He took Jennie's light. "I bet we'll see hoof marks here."

He raked the dim light across the entrance to the lane. Miranda and Jennie crowded close. No hoofprints were to be seen.

"I *told* you!" Miranda said triumphantly.

"There's some logical explanation," Bill insisted. "It must have been running in the grass where we can't see the marks."

Miranda said stubbornly, "It was in the air."

"Then how come we heard hoofbeats?" demanded Bill.

"I don't know." Miranda sounded close to tears.

Jennie put a comforting hand on her arm. Probably Miranda did think she had seen a horse in the air. After Grandma Mitchell's stories tonight a person might imagine anything.

She tried to think logically. "Do you know anyone around here who has horses?"

"Not nearby," said Bill. "But there's Harvey's Stables on Upper Mountain Road. And my horse and Fair Lady . . ."

Jennie cut in. "Do you suppose Cloud or Fair Lady could've gotten out?"

"I don't see how." Bill's steps quickened. "But I'm going to take a look."

Bill, Jennie, and Miranda went past the Fred Mitchell house on the run. The garage was still empty.

Though her flashlight was getting fainter by the minute, Jennie kept it on, checking the sides of the road for hoofprints.

Again the wind rose, stronger than before. The branches of the trees thrashed the air until Jennie was afraid they would be struck by broken limbs. Halfway home, the flashlight gave out completely.

Running and walking by turns, the three sped up the road. The noise of the wind and the creaking of the trees would have made conversation difficult anyway, but they were saving their breath for running.

At last they reached Bill's house. Just beyond it, Bill jumped the narrow ditch at the side of the road and cut across to the rutted driveway that led through the field to the barn.

Jennie and Miranda hurried after him, stumbling in the dark. Soon the barn loomed up ahead of them, a dim bulk against the dark sky.

Bill flung open the wide door and the two girls followed him inside. A warm, horsy smell greeted them and Jennie heard the stamp of hoofs on the thick straw bedding that covered the concrete floor. At least one horse was in the barn, but in the darkness she couldn't tell more than that.

Something soft rubbed against her ankles and she was alarmed until she realized it was only Eagle Eye, the tomcat that stayed in the barn. A zealous mouser, he lived well on the mice that were attracted by the hay and grain stored in the loft.

Bill spoke from a few feet away. "They're both here," he said. "They aren't heated up or breathing hard. They haven't been out tonight, I'm sure of that. I was afraid some kid might have taken one of them out for a ride." He blew a sigh of relief. "I'd be in for it if anything happened to Fair Lady. Gordon Trent thinks she's the greatest. Can't say I blame him."

"She's the best-looking horse I ever saw," Jennie agreed. Her heart was still pounding from her run. "Is she valuable? You know, would someone think she's worth stealing?"

"Sure. I don't know exactly how much she's worth, but probably a lot. She's fast and well-trained and she has papers that trace her blood lines back a long way. She has brought home blue ribbons from horse shows. Besides," Bill added, "a good Western saddle like hers with all that silver on it is worth two or three thousand dollars, maybe more."

Jennie realized that Miranda was no longer at her side. "Miranda, where are you?" she called.

"Over here with Fair Lady," came the answer. "She likes to have me rub her nose."

Bill chuckled. "You and that horse. You sure talk the same language."

"So the horse we heard wasn't Cloud or Fair Lady," commented Jennie. "Funny that anyone would be out riding tonight. It's so dark. A horse might step in a hole and fall."

"Y'know, it was strange the way that sound came right at us. Weird." Bill drew a deep breath. "There's a common-sense answer if we could figure it out."

Jennie laughed softly. "I hate to tell you, but I thought of the Flying Heads. Of course, I guess that was because Grandma was talking about them tonight."

"Ask your grandmother what she thinks about that horse we heard," suggested Bill. "She's a wise woman— even if she doesn't understand about your wanting to go to college."

"I know," said Jennie. "People are always coming to her for advice." Jennie felt as if she had been disloyal. She had been angry with Grandma, even though she hadn't said anything against her. And what would she do without her grandmother? Ever since her mother had died ten years ago, she had lived with her grandparents. Her father had never remarried, and Jennie rarely saw him. Soon after his wife's death, he had moved to Detroit where he worked on high steel construction. He sent money regularly for her and once in a while he phoned, but he had turned her over to Grandma and Grandpa Mitchell to raise.

Jennie called to Miranda, "We'd better go home." Now that they had reached the barn, Miranda seemed to have forgotten her desire to go to sleep.

As she stepped outside and looked toward home, Jennie saw to her dismay that lights were blazing all over the house. Grandma and Grandpa must have awakened and started to look for her and Miranda.

"Come on," she urged. "We're in for it."

"*I* wanted to come home ages ago," Miranda said as they ran down the path.

Grandpa Mitchell heard them coming and met them at the back door.

"The prodigals are home," he said in his gentle way. "We were worried about you."

Jennie knew that was all he would have to say. He was never one to scold. "I'm sorry, Grandpa," she apologized.

Grandma Mitchell burst into the kitchen. Her dark eyes were flashing and her five-foot, one-inch form seemed to fill the room.

Miranda didn't wait for Mrs. Mitchell to speak. "Wait till you hear what we saw tonight!" she exclaimed.

"I can wait," said Grandma, "until I hear where you two went this time of night."

Jennie took over. "It's my fault. I couldn't find Miranda so I went out to look for her."

"And I was on the porch all the time," said Miranda, "until Dan told me Jennie had gone down the road."

"Then we both went with Bill to see if his canoe was safe," Jennie concluded.

If Grandma was confused by this explanation, she didn't show it. "Why didn't you tell me you were going?"

"I didn't want to wake you up," said Jennie.

"Next time, wake me. I was about ready to call the police. Do you realize it's past midnight?" She shifted her intent gaze to Miranda. "Now what did you see?"

"A horse, up in the sky."

Grandma pulled out a chair and sat down at the kitchen table. "A horse?" she asked. "In the sky?"

"Bill and I didn't see it," said Jennie. "We heard hoofbeats and a whinny, though. They seemed to start over by Uncle Fred's and they got louder and louder, as if they were coming across Lake Etmejejo right to us."

"But you didn't see the horse," said Grandma.

"Not a thing."

"Jennie and Bill didn't look high enough." Miranda's blue eyes shone.

"Exactly what did you see?" Grandma seemed half-amused. "One of those Flying Heads I told you about?"

Miranda pulled herself up straighter and looked Grandma directly in the eyes. "I saw a horse with an enormous head and a skeleton body. He went right over us."

Grandma no longer looked amused. "Now, young lady, we've had enough of this nonsense. Who told you about this skeleton horse?"

Miranda looked frightened. "No one. I saw it, I tell you!"

"Jennie, did you tell her?" demanded Grandma.

"I never heard of a horse like that," said Jennie.

"There *was* a horse like that, a ghost horse." Grandma's voice was almost a whisper. "It came more than a hundred years ago to warn our people of trouble that was coming. Right after it was seen a terrible epidemic killed almost everyone in the tribe. My grandmother told me about it."

Grandpa spoke up. "That was a long time ago, Sarah. Ghosts don't come around any more."

Grandma looked up at her husband, and Jennie could

see that her eyes were sad. "What do we know about ghosts or witches?" she asked. "We don't live close to the earth the way our ancestors did. The spirits may be all around us and we're too blind to see them and too deaf to hear."

Jennie shifted from one foot to another and looked with longing toward the stairs. She wanted to escape when Grandma started talking like this. She didn't want to believe in spirits—and yet Grandma sounded so sure, it was hard not to believe.

Grandpa shuffled across the room in his felt slippers to close the kitchen door. "It's late. Let's go to bed."

But Grandma remained motionless on the hard kitchen chair. "Nat, I'm scared," she told him. "Jennie said the sound of the horse started near Fred's house. What if we've chosen the wrong chief? Maybe the ghost horse is telling us we've made a mistake."

CHAPTER
5

For a moment there was silence in the kitchen.

Then Jennie exclaimed, "Oh, no!"

Nathaniel Mitchell's weathered face looked drawn. "Sarah, think what you're saying!" he cried. Then he added more quietly, "Even if Miranda did see a ghost horse—which I doubt—why should it warn us about the chief you've chosen? He's a good man."

Jennie noticed how careful he was not to mention Uncle Fred's name.

"I know it," replied Grandma. "But you heard Jennie say where the sound started. That's an omen. And who heard it? My own grandchild and *his* favorite niece."

Jennie's mind leaped rapidly from one idea to another. Why should Miranda pretend she had seen a ghost horse? How terrible to have Uncle Fred lose his chance to be a chief through no fault of his own. *Was* she his favorite niece? He was her favorite uncle, she was sure of that.

"Grandma, I know that wasn't a ghost horse we heard tonight," she said earnestly. "Bill said sound carries fast on a night like this, especially across water."

"You forget, Miranda *saw* it," Sarah Mitchell reminded her.

"She might have been mistaken." Jennie looked toward Miranda, hoping she would agree. "It was foggy tonight. Maybe she saw some mist or even a bird and thought it was a horse."

"No," Miranda declared. "I told you what I saw." She left the kitchen abruptly and Jennie heard her running up the stairs.

Grandma said wearily, "I would think she was imagining things if she hadn't given a perfect description of the ghost horse that gave the warning about the epidemic. And I don't see how she could do that when she never heard of it."

"The ghost horse came just once to warn of a terrible catastrophe that affected all our tribe," Grandpa reminded his wife. "It wouldn't come because of one man."

"But one man—one chief—can have an effect on many people. Think of Ganiodaiyo—Handsome Lake—and how great his influence is. Many Indians are guided today by the good code he gave the Iroquois Nations over a hundred years ago." Grandma pushed her chair back. "Let's go to bed. Tomorrow I must call the women together and tell them about it. They should have the chance to pick another chief if they want to."

"Don't—" Grandpa picked up an empty glass and carried it to the sink. Jennie noticed with dismay that his hand was shaking. Even though he had been retired from his factory job for several years, she had never thought of him as old. Yet, at this moment he looked like an old man. "Don't tell anyone about it tomorrow," he said. "Think about it for a few days."

Grandma shook her head. "I feel as bad about it as you do, Nat, but supposing we went ahead with it and something happened to the new chief? We'd never forgive ourselves."

Jennie had an inspiration. "You know the people who heard the ghost horse a long time ago—" she began.

"Yes." Grandma's dark eyes took on a far-off expression, as if they could penetrate the years.

"Those people didn't know why it had come," Jennie went on. "We don't know, either! If a ghost horse was here tonight we don't know what it came to warn us about. Even if it was near Uncle Fred's, it might have come to tell us not to eat the cherries this year or that the fish in Lake Etmejejo aren't good—or anything!"

This argument seemed to have an effect. Jennie's grandmother turned around in the doorway. "That's true," she said thoughtfully. "I'll wait a day before I talk to the women. Maybe the reason for this omen will come clear."

"Make it a week," her husband pleaded.

"A day," Grandma replied firmly.

"Until after the picnic, anyway," said Grandpa. The annual Tuscarora picnic was two days away.

"Well—all right," she agreed reluctantly.

Jennie went slowly up the stairs. Grandpa didn't believe in the ghost horse. Perhaps that was because he had been out in the world more than Grandma. Everything Jennie had learned in school and church denied the existence of ghosts and witches. The more she thought about it, the more convinced she was that Miranda's imagination had tricked her or she had for some reason made up the story of the skeleton horse.

In the bedroom Miranda, still fully dressed, was standing by the open window. She turned around as Jennie came in. "No rain yet, but I heard thunder off that way." She pointed to the east.

"The storm may be going around us," said Jennie. She sat down wearily on the edge of the cot and pulled off her sneakers.

Miranda flung back the hand-pieced quilt that served as a bedspread. "I'm so *tired!* I don't think I'll even brush my teeth."

"After all that sleep on the porch?" asked Jennie.

Miranda was removing her torn pink slacks. She rolled them into a ball and tossed them onto the closet floor before she answered.

"Just the same, I'm tired," she said defensively.

Jennie wished she could read what was going on inside that tousled blonde head.

"Miranda," she begged. "Something's wrong. Can't you tell me?"

Miranda dropped onto her bed and gave Jennie a blank, blue-eyed stare. "Nothing's wrong." It was as if she put a wall between herself and her friend.

"You don't act the same. And your slacks—I notice they're torn."

"I fell when I ran down the road after you."

In spite of her grandmother's teaching, Jennie persisted. Something was at stake that was more important than good manners.

"Miranda, you know what a great honor it is to be chosen a chief. Why, it's like being a senator. The chiefs have a council and they settle problems and make rules for the good of the reservation. Everyone respects them."

Miranda squirmed. "You don't have to give me a lecture."

Jennie went to Miranda's bed and sat down beside her. "You know the one who was chosen. He'd be such a wonderful chief, but he may never be one if Grandma keeps on believing you saw a ghost horse."

"I'm too tired to argue about it," Miranda said stubbornly. "I don't know why you won't believe me."

Jennie jumped up from the bed. She was too angry to say another word. In silence she undressed and washed. But just as she turned off the light, Miranda said in a muffled voice, "Don't be cross with me, Jennie. You're the best friend I ever had."

"How can I help being cross?" demanded Jennie.

Miranda began to cry, and Jennie relented. "All right, I forgive you. But—don't you see—it's so important. If you have even a little doubt about the ghost horse, please tell Grandma."

For some time she continued to hear an occasional sniffle from the other bed, but long after Miranda's sobs had stopped, Jennie was still awake. The wind blew in gusts that sent the curtains billowing into the room and rattled the television antenna on top of the house. But still the rain did not come.

She lay wide-eyed on the cot and tried to figure out how she could convince Grandma that it was not a ghost horse she, Bill, and Miranda had heard that night. She, herself, couldn't understand how Miranda had known the way to describe the ghost horse. And why would she lie about it?

Looking back over the years, Jennie realized that Grandma had always believed in spirits. Probably it was because she was a clan mother and it was her job to keep alive the old legends and traditions. Then, too, Grandma's father and mother had brought her up in many of the old beliefs.

In the bed across the room Miranda was asleep, judging by the deep, even rhythm of her breathing. Jennie thought sadly of the times when they had told each other their problems and secret thoughts. Where had that Miranda gone?

Tomorrow, decided Jennie, first thing, I'll tell Bill

how Grandma believes Miranda's story and that Uncle Fred may lose his chance to be a chief. Maybe he'll be able to figure a way out of this mess. Her walk with Bill that night had made her like him more than ever. He was a person you could depend on, she was sure.

And he liked the way she looked. She put her hand to her face and touched her wide cheekbones with a sense of discovery. Tonight, with Bill, she had felt so good, so *whole*. It reminded her of the times when she had gazed at the sky and felt on the verge of entering a new and wonderful world.

Jennie awakened at eight o'clock. Miranda's bed was empty, and that was surprising, because she liked to sleep late.

Stretching and yawning, Jennie went to the window through which sunlight was streaming. The storm that had by-passed them had left the air less humid, though still hot.

From the window Jennie could see the small barn where Fair Lady and Cloud were housed, its gray, shingled roof shining in the sun. As she watched, Miranda came through the doorway leading Fair Lady. A moment later she mounted and disappeared behind the barn.

Jennie was puzzled. She knew Miranda had ridden Fair Lady several times, but always when Gordon Trent had been there. Had he given her permission to ride whenever she wished? He had seemed happy that she liked his filly. Still, it was strange that Miranda hadn't mentioned that Gordon had said she could ride at any time.

In spite of her doubts, Jennie was pleased that Miranda would be away for a while. This would give her an opportunity to talk alone with Bill about the ghost horse.

Perhaps, she thought as she ran downstairs, Grandma had changed her mind by now.

But this morning Grandma was even more convinced than she had been the night before that Miranda had seen a ghost horse. She looked tired and admitted she hadn't slept well.

"I shouldn't have promised to wait till after the picnic," she fumed. "The sooner we start choosing a new chief, the better."

"Don't you want *him* to be a chief?" asked Jennie. She couldn't understand why Grandma was in such a hurry to call the women together. Usually she believed in taking time before making an important decision.

"Of course I want the chosen one to be the chief," Grandma answered. "He's a good man and he'd be a fine chief. At least *I* think so. But now that the ghost horse has given us a warning, we have no time to waste. Some harm may come to all of us."

Jennie studied her grandmother's face as she never had before and she saw something there she did not usually see. Fear lurked in the dark eyes. Grandma wasn't fooling about this. It was as if she had finally received a sign she had been awaiting and dreading.

"Where did Miranda go?" Jennie asked. "I saw her on Fair Lady."

"She's exercising Mr. Trent's horse. She said she knew it was all right with him." Grandma frowned. "I don't like her going off alone like that. Supposing that horse throws her?"

"Miranda's a good rider," said Jennie. She, too, felt uneasy. Exercising Fair Lady was supposed to be Bill's job.

She swallowed her breakfast hastily and went to the phone to call Bill.

"We have a new problem about the horse we heard last night," she told him. "Could we talk about it?"

"Sure," he replied. "Meet me at the barn. We'll take the horses out for a trot and we can talk while we ride."

"Fair Lady's out. Miranda went across the field with her about half an hour ago. She told Grandma that she was sure Gordon wouldn't mind if she exercised his filly."

After a moment of silence Bill said, "How about that! He didn't tell me she could. Oh, well, she knows how to handle that horse. I'll be right over, Jennie."

"Fine," said Jennie. Her usual after-breakfast hour of piano practice would have to be postponed today.

Grandpa had heard Jennie talking on the phone. He looked up from the paper he was reading and said gravely, "Good luck, Jennie."

She wanted to run over and hug him, but she knew he would be embarrassed. He and Grandma didn't show their affection in that way, but in day by day kindnesses.

In less than five minutes Bill was at the door. Before she had time to say a word, he said, "Let's go down to the lane. I don't think we looked far enough last night, and your flashlight was as good as nothing. The more I think of it, the lane's the only place the horse could have been. Remember how the hoofbeats sounded? As if they were on hard-packed ground or grass. Not pavement."

Jennie considered this. "I don't know how they sounded. I was too scared at the time. But let's go look."

"I don't believe Miranda's flying-horse story for a minute," Bill went on as they started toward the road. "And I don't like having someone try to put the blinders on me. I'm going to prove she was making that up if it's the last thing I do."

"Wait till you hear what happened when I got home," said Jennie. "Now we have another reason for proving we heard a real horse." As they walked down the road toward the lane, she recounted Grandma's reaction to Miranda's report of having seen a skeleton horse in the air.

As he listened, Bill's face became more and more troubled. "Bad." He shook his head: "It's bad. Till after the picnic, that's as long as your grandmother will wait?"

Jennie nodded. "Bill, how could Miranda know about the kind of ghost horse she described? She isn't an Indian, and I guess not many Indians even know about it.

I never heard about a horse with a huge head and a skeleton body."

"She heard about it someplace," said Bill. "You can be sure of that. Or it was a lucky guess on her part. Now listen. If we can find a few hoofprints in the lane, even if they're not at the entrance, maybe we can show them to your grandmother and she'll realize it was a live horse we heard."

He's right, thought Jennie. Bill's steady brown eyes and calm voice reassured her.

They hurried unseeing down the road, beside the marsh where a red-winged blackbird balanced on a cattail, past a grove of tall pine and maple trees that made the roadway cool. Now and then a car whizzed past, but Bill and Jennie were so intent on their problem, they did not even look up to see if they knew the occupants.

The entrance to the lane basked in sunshine. The dirt road was dry and dusty except for one deep rut that Jennie had noticed always contained a puddle.

"Keep your eyes . . ." began Bill. But he broke off in mid-sentence, for at once he and Jennie saw the marks of horseshoes in the dirt.

"Those tracks weren't there last night," said Jennie. "I'm sure of it."

"So am I." Bill stared glumly at the hoofprints.

"Someone's been here today."

As they stared at the ground, they heard the sound of distant hoofbeats coming down the lane toward them.

Bill raised his hand, cautioning silence. "That's the same sound we heard last night, isn't it?"

"Yes, only there's no whinny."

Bill started down the lane. "Let's go to meet that horse. It may sound the same as last night, but I have a hunch it's a different rider."

CHAPTER
6

As soon as Bill and Jennie entered the lane, the heat closed in on them. Not a breath of wind stirred. On their right a second-growth woodland extended for one hundred feet to the top of the ridge. On the left side of the lane mountain ash, blackberry bushes, and tall weeds fringed the road. The air seemed to pulsate and hum with warmth and insect voices.

Bill slapped too late at a mosquito. A welt began to rise on his bare forearm.

"How come I'm the one that gets bitten?" he asked, rubbing his arm. "Girls are supposed to be more tender."

"Even a mosquito can make a mistake," replied Jennie. She appreciated his attempt at humor. The situation was all too grim. She was afraid these fresh hoofprints had trampled their best hope for proving Miranda was wrong. And she, too, had a strong suspicion about who was on the horse.

The scent of ripe cherries reached them, and soon

they were walking between rows of trees heavy with fruit almost ready to pick. Some branches sagged to the ground.

"Next week we'll have plenty of work," Bill commented.

"Miranda and I have already promised to pick," said Jennie.

The approaching horse was now near at hand, moving at a walk. Jennie and Bill crossed a belt of shade where a beech tree threw a deep shadow. On their right the woods were dense on the ridge and down the slope to the edge of the Lower Mountain Road. The distance between the lane and the top of the ridge was wider at this point. Glancing into the shadows, Jennie noticed a narrow opening that led into a grassy clearing. What a perfect place for a picnic, she thought. She and Miranda and Bill could bring a lunch and eat there some noon when they were picking cherries.

When she looked along the lane she saw Fair Lady and Miranda rounding a bend a short distance ahead of them. Jennie felt no surprise.

Bill exclaimed, "I thought so!"

Horse and rider continued toward them, at the same steady gait. Annoyed though she was with Miranda, Jennie couldn't help noticing what a splendid picture they made. Miranda rode straight and slim with her blonde head shining in the sun, while the black filly she rode had the proud bearing of a champion. Fair Lady's four white feet lifted rhythmically and she was so clean and well brushed she glistened. As she neared Bill and Jennie, she bowed her head as if in greeting and whinnied softly.

It was a far pleasanter sound than the wild whinny they had heard the night before.

"Hi, slowpokes!" Miranda called out. "I've been doing your work for you today, Bill!"

Bill was in no mood to be distracted. "Who said you could take that filly out?" he demanded.

"Well, nobody, but Gordon wouldn't care."

"I'm not so sure about that," said Bill. He continued with some heat. "And why did you come to this lane to ride? You know horses aren't supposed to come here, especially when the cherries are ripe. And we wanted to look for hoofprints in the lane. Now if there were any you've covered them up. Is that what you were trying to do? So we'd believe your big story about a ghost horse?"

Miranda's face crumpled. "I was trying to help! I thought you'd be so glad I exercised Fair Lady for you!" She began to cry. "I saddled her myself and everything!"

Bill frowned. "Aw, stop crying. I'm sorry I hurt your feelings."

Miranda wiped her eyes on her sleeve and looked pleadingly at him. Jennie was surprised to discover that she felt sorry for her. She seemed so little and helpless up there. A girl her age wouldn't cry like that if she didn't feel terrible. Maybe she was ill.

"She didn't mean anything wrong," said Jennie.

Miranda gave her a grateful look.

Bill thrust his hands into his pockets and hunched his shoulders. "I suppose not. Miranda, did you see any hoofprints when you went up the lane? Any that Fair Lady didn't make?"

Miranda gave him a blank look. "You just said horses aren't supposed to come here, so there wouldn't be any prints, would there?"

Bill stared at her with doubt in his eyes. "There's nothing to keep them out if someone like you decides to ride in here. Generally speaking, we Indians know what a 'No Trespassing' sign means."

Miranda's face fell again. "You're still cross," she said in a whisper.

"I sure am. Come on, Jennie. No use our staying around here," he said.

Miranda said meekly, "I'll go right back across the fields the way I came. That's safer for Fair Lady than the road."

As she and Bill started back, Jennie said, "I think you're too hard on her. She didn't know we wanted to look for signs of a horse."

"I'm not so sure about that." Bill's mouth was set in a firm line. "You'd think she'd tell the truth when your grandmother said she was going to have the women choose another chief. Doesn't she like your uncle?"

"She likes him a lot."

Bill sighed. "I don't understand it at all."

As they passed Fred Mitchell's house, just to the right of the lane, Jennie's uncle rose from the steps and called out in Tuscarora, "*Chwad!*"

Bill replied, "*Chwad!* Even I know that means hello."

Fred gave him a mock salute and said, "Jennie, can you stay and help me a while? I'd like to work on the book till noon."

"All right, Bill?" asked Jennie.

"Of course. I'll see you after lunch." Bill shoved his hands into his pockets and strode away.

As Jennie went up the front walk, she wondered how she could act natural with her uncle, knowing of the storm that was brewing around him.

He led the way to the living room, and though Jennie went at once to the big shabby desk at the far end of the narrow room, he began to pace up and down. That was a sign that he was thinking hard about something, for he always paced when he was wrestling with a problem. It was amazing, Jennie thought, that he had chosen to work on a book, for he was an outdoorsman. She had often seen him run in a game of lacrosse until it seemed impossible that he could stand. And then he would walk home because he preferred that to riding in a car.

He had begun the unfamiliar task of writing a children's school book only because of his conviction that the young Tuscaroras should learn to read and speak their own language. For centuries the Tuscarora language had been passed down by word of mouth. Now it had been recorded and the children were studying it in school. One of the women of the reservation who had learned the language from her mother and father was teaching it. Unfortunately, there were few books for the students to read. Fred Mitchell hoped to give them stories that would contain information about their Indian heritage.

As he passed a window, the light caught the wartime scar on his left cheek. He had been a captain in the infantry. The scar did not spoil the lean handsomeness of his face, Jennie observed with warm affection.

What a good chief he would be! The boys he had coached in basketball and lacrosse liked and admired him. Old people liked him, too, and he gave them the respect due to age. How could Grandma think of having his name canceled?

As she took out paper and pencil, Jennie tried to put the problems of the ghost horse and the chieftainship from her thoughts.

Still pacing, Uncle Fred began to dictate the story he was adding to the Tuscarora reader that day. If he had anything else on his mind, he apparently wasn't going to tell her about it. He seemed to be absorbed only in the problem of telling about Nicholas Cusick, one of the Tuscaroras who had helped the colonists in the American Revolution.

"Cusick was an aide to General Lafayette and many times risked his own life to protect Lafayette," Uncle Fred dictated.

"After the war he could have received a government pension, but the law required that he swear he couldn't live without the pension money. Nicholas couldn't do this. He said, 'Now here is my little cabin, and it is my own; here is my patch of ground where I raise my corn and beans and there is Lake Oneida where I can fish; with these I can make out to live without the pension, and to say that I could not would be a lie to the Great Spirit.' "

Jennie could hear her aunt and the three children talking in the kitchen, but she knew they wouldn't come into the living room while she and her uncle were working. She longed to ask them if they had heard a horse last night, but she was afraid to say anything for fear they would start questioning her.

Shortly before noon, Fred Mitchell declared they had done enough for the day. He went outdoors with her and sat on the front steps in the sun.

"How are things with you, Jennie?" he asked. "Sometimes when I'm out for a walk I hear you practicing your piano or guitar or your clarinet. I like to hear you. You have a gift."

"Enough of a gift so I should go on to college?" she asked, sitting down beside him.

"I'd say yes."

"Grandma says no. No college, that is."

"I know." His thin face showed little expression, but his dark eyes were understanding. "Patience," he said. "Time has a way of making things come right."

Time again, thought Jennie. Time doesn't always work magic the way everyone thinks it will. "I can't wait much longer," she said. "I only have till the middle of August to change my classes. If I'm going to college I have to start a college entrance program this fall."

"I know . . ." He stopped abruptly, and Jennie knew he had been about to tell her something. When he went on, he said only, "You still have a month. Things will work out." He leaned back on his elbows and closed his eyes. "This sun makes me sleepy."

Jennie smiled. "No wonder. You must've been working late last night. Your car was gone when I passed here close to midnight."

He opened his eyes and looked thoughtfully at her. "I wasn't working last night, but I was out. In fact, all of us were out. I had an appointment, and I dropped Milly and the kids at her sister's."

Jennie asked no questions. Uncle Fred had said he was "out" and that was all that was necessary. It was his business where he was. It was so much a part of her training that she didn't have to remind herself not to pry. "Indians don't ask personal questions," Grandma had taught her.

Through the open door she heard the radio in the kitchen come on with the midday news report from one of the Niagara Falls stations. She and Uncle Fred fell silent, listening.

As soon as the news is over, I'll go home, she thought. The reporter's voice droned on, and Jennie's attention drifted. The mayor and the council were at odds on some point. A record number of tourists had visited the Falls the day before. A news bulletin just received . . . a valuable mare had disappeared from the Harvey Riding Stables on the Tuscarora Reservation. Apparently she had been stolen.

Suddenly Jennie was alert. The Harvey Riding Stables on the Upper Mountain Road were not far from where she lived. Pete Campbell, the redheaded boy who had used Bill's canoe, worked there.

An idea leaped into Jennie's mind. The stolen mare could have been the horse they had heard last night!

She decided not to wait for the end of the news report. With a wave of her hand, she ran down the walk and hurried toward home. This should convince Grandma that the mysterious horse was no ghost.

CHAPTER
7

Jennie was passing the swamp where the cattails grew when she saw Bill Tomilsin coming down the road toward her.

"Did you hear the news report?" she asked excitedly.

"I did. That's why I came after you. Hurry up and eat so we can go over to Harvey's Stables."

"What if Miranda wants to come?"

"Let her. She and I had a long talk this morning while you were at your uncle's. I decided I ought to try to understand her, the way you do. I think she wants attention. It was hard on her losing her mother and stepfather both at the same time like that," Bill said sympathetically, "and she says her aunt is always busy. Even when she's home she's usually correcting papers or writing lectures, so Miranda leads a lonely life."

"That's right," said Jennie. "We ought to do everything we can to help her be happy this summer. Did she tell you about her stepbrother?"

"Yes—Gary. I gather she likes him but he's moved away so she never sees him." Bill turned in at the Tomilsin house. "I'll see you in a few minutes."

Jennie burst eagerly into the kitchen with her news of the stolen mare. Grandma Mitchell was alone, preparing lunch. She, too, had been listening to the radio.

"This proves it was no ghost horse we heard!" exclaimed Jennie. "Doesn't it?"

Grandma set a bowl of raspberries on the table. "Not necessarily. There could have been two horses out last night—a live one and the ghost horse."

"Oh, Grandma—don't say that!" Jennie was disheartened.

"I'd like to believe you heard a real horse," said Grandma, "but you don't even know which way that mare went."

"If we could prove it was on the lane near Lake Etmejejo, then would you believe?" But how can I prove that? she wondered.

Grandma cocked her head to one side. "That depends, Jennie. I can see you think the ghost horse is just an old lady's idea. But when you've lived as long as I have, you'll realize that science can't explain everything. Many, many times in our history the spirits helped our people."

"They don't seem to help any more," said Jennie. "I never hear about any spirits coming around. And look what a hard time Indians have. We're poor and we get driven off our lands." She thought how only a few years before land had been taken from the Tuscaroras to make a reservoir for the big Niagara Falls power project.

"As I said before," Grandma went on, "we're too far away from nature. Once every tree and flower and blade of grass was our brother." She spread her small, work-hardened hands as if blessing the earth. "We were grateful for the gifts we received. My mother always gave thanks for the first berries every summer and the first corn. Not many do that now."

Jennie was moved by her grandmother's words, but she recognized an error in her thinking. "Miranda isn't an Indian," she pointed out. "Why should she see the ghost horse? Grandma, I think Miranda must have imagined it."

"Then how did she know how to describe it?"

They were back to that again.

Jennie admitted, "I don't know. But she must have heard about it someplace." A slight noise in the doorway made her look up to see Miranda standing there. "Please, Miranda," she begged, "tell Grandma the truth about last night. It's terribly important."

Miranda's face turned pink, but she said firmly, "I told you what I saw. What else can I do?"

Jennie recognized by her grandmother's expression that she believed Miranda. Grandma was so good and honest herself she sometimes had too much faith in people.

Suddenly Jennie had an inspiration. "I'm going to phone Miss Hugo!" she announced.

Miss Hugo had made a study of Tuscarora legends and history, and she was the one who had suggested that Miranda might spend the summer with the Mitchells. Probably *she* had told Miranda about the ghost horse.

Miranda appeared unconcerned. "Go ahead. It won't do you any good. She never talked to me about Tuscarora history or anything like that."

Jennie went straight to the phone. Miss Hugo lived in Buffalo, so it would be a toll call, but it would be worth it. She would pay for it from her own allowance. Excitedly she waited for Miss Hugo to lift the receiver. To her disappointment, there was no response to the repeated ringing.

With a sigh she gave up. "Bill and I are going to the Harvey Stables after lunch," she told Miranda. "Want to go along?"

Miranda was delighted. "Oh, yes! Maybe we'll find out more about that mare they lost!"

"You heard about it, then," said Jennie.

"Just a few minutes ago on the radio. The poor little colt must be so lonely."

"Did a colt disappear, too? I didn't hear the whole report."

"No, just a mare. A gorgeous horse named Venus. She has a colt."

Bill was outside the barn with the horses saddled and ready when Jennie and Miranda finished their hasty lunch.

"Miranda, you ride Fair Lady, and Jennie, take Cloud. I'll run. Good practice for me," he said.

Miranda needed no second invitation to mount Fair Lady.

Jennie liked Cloud. He was a pinto and not as beautiful as Fair Lady, but he was a good, steady gelding. She climbed happily onto his back and gathered up the reins.

They cut across the field behind the house and headed southwest, in the direction of the Upper Mountain Road. In this way they approached the Harvey Riding Stables from the rear.

In a large fenced-in field behind the stables several horses were nibbling at the grass or trotting idly around.

At once Jennie saw Pete Campbell's red hair. The young man had a bucket of food from which he was trying to persuade a leggy brown-and-white colt to eat. The colt did not seem interested.

Bill called out, "Hi, Pete!"

Pete set the pail on the grass and joined them at the fence. "You hear about Venus?" he asked.

Jennie was struck by his pallor. Beneath the short red hair his freckles stood out in his white face. His skin never tanned well, but today he looked sick.

"We heard it on the noon news," Bill said. "What happened?"

Pete leaned on the fence. "We're still trying to find out. She disappeared during the night. Must have been stolen. She'd never jump the fence and run away without her colt. Look at him. He's so lonesome for her he won't eat. Good thing he's pretty well weaned."

"Any clues?"

"Not that I know of. Mr. Harvey called the troopers. One's here now, over in the office. Harvey's mad at me." Pete rubbed his hand over his freckled face.

"Why?" asked Bill. "I don't see how you could help it. You don't even stay here nights, do you?"

"No. I have a room downtown at the Falls. I leave here right after I feed the horses at about 7:00 P.M. He's mad at me because I didn't tell him right away this morning that Venus was missing."

Jennie could understand Mr. Harvey's annoyance. "Why didn't you?"

"I thought Mr. Harvey's son had taken Venus before I got here this morning, or maybe even last night after I left. He does it all the time, though he hasn't done it since Venus had the colt. I've told him he ought to let me know, but he never paid any attention to me." He added bitterly, "I'm just the hired man around here."

"So today Harvey's son didn't have Venus," prompted Bill.

"Yeah, and I'm in the doghouse." Pete groaned and leaned his head in his hands. He was a picture of misery.

Bill said gruffly, "I shouldn't jump on you when you're down, but I wish you'd leave my canoe alone. I had to wade out in the lake for it last night."

Pete looked even more uncomfortable. "What makes you think I had it?"

"I had a report," said Bill. "You can't get away with anything with that red hair. You were using the canoe yesterday, weren't you?"

Pete straightened and met Bill's eyes. "Sure. I didn't think you'd mind." He glanced over his shoulder toward the long white stable. "Oh, oh. Here they come."

A tall state trooper in gray uniform came toward them, accompanied by a lean, tanned, middle-aged man whom Jennie recognized as Mr. Harvey, the owner of the stables.

She wondered if they should leave, but Bill put his hand on Cloud's bridle and said quietly, "We'd better tell the trooper about the horse we heard last night."

Cloud and Fair Lady waited patiently. Jennie liked the warm feel of the horse's body against her knees, the sense of being accepted by the animal. She patted his neck now and then as she listened to the men.

Mr. Harvey was angry. His face was flushed and his eyes were too brilliant as he said, "This is my groom, Pete Campbell. Didn't tell me Venus was missing till late this morning."

"I told you why, Mr. Harvey," Pete protested.

The trooper said quietly, "Yes, Mr. Harvey told me." He had an open notebook in his hand and he began at once to question Pete. "Did you notice any breaks in the fence or anything unusual that would show where the mare was taken out?"

"No, sir. There's a gate in the fence, front and back. This back gate leads to the trail the riders take after they've had enough practice in the ring. And the front gate—well, you came through that."

"No lock on the gates, I suppose?"

"That's right. We never had to worry about thieves, and the horses can't open the gates themselves."

The trooper's eyes flicked toward Bill, Jennie, and Miranda. "You know anything about this?"

Bill spoke up. "Yes, sir. At least, there was a horse making a racket last night. We were down by Lake Etmejejo and we heard hoofbeats and a lot of whinnying."

"Did you see the horse?" asked the trooper.

Bill said, "No. We were on the north side of the lake and it sounded as if the horse was at the top of the hill. In fact, it seemed to go right over our heads, but I think that was because of the way sound carries across water."

Jennie wondered if Miranda would tell the trooper she had seen a horse flying in the air, but to her relief Miranda kept still.

"Thanks," said the trooper. "We'll see if anyone else saw or heard a horse last night." He had not put down any notes on Bill's information. Jennie had the impression he didn't think it was important.

The trooper turned to Pete Campbell. "Have you seen anyone hanging around, watching the horses? Anyone acting suspicious?"

Pete rubbed the side of his nose. "Only one I can think of is a Sioux Indian who comes around most every day.

He's new around here. Seems to be crazy about horses."

"Come to think of it, I've seen a big fellow hanging around a lot," said Mr. Harvey. "Must be the one you're talking about. He looks like a western Indian."

"What's his name?" The trooper had his notebook ready for this.

"Dan Gray Wolf," Pete told him. "Lives in that tan-colored trailer on the left-hand side between here and Blacknose Spring Road."

Bill burst out, "Dan's OK. I know him and he's no horse thief. He goes to college in Buffalo and this summer he's working on the Rainbow Bridge. Painting it."

Jennie shuddered as she thought of Dan painting the huge bridge that connected the cities of Niagara Falls, U.S.A., and Niagara Falls, Canada. How did he dare climb around on those metal girders high above the tumbling Niagara River? Oh, well, it was probably no worse than her father's work on Detroit skyscrapers. Most Indians were sure-footed and didn't mind heights.

The trooper wrote Dan's name and closed his notebook. He met Bill's eyes. "If this Sioux is the kind of fellow you say, he won't mind answering a question or two."

Mr. Harvey and the trooper walked away.

When they were out of earshot, Bill demanded, "Hey, Pete, why'd you have to mention Dan? You know he's all right."

Pete picked up the pail of food the colt had ignored.

"How do I know he's all right? Like I said, he's around here all the time." He started to walk away, then he turned around to add, "Look, I'm not protecting any-body. I want to see Venus back here. So does that colt."

CHAPTER
8

Jennie looked at Venus' colt. He was standing motion-less with his head drooping. At a glance anyone could tell he was sad.

Suddenly Miranda, who had dismounted, climbed over the fence and ran after Pete.

"Give me that pail!" she called. "Let me try to get the colt to eat."

Pete thrust the pail into her hands. "Good luck!"

Jennie and Bill watched while Miranda put her arms around the colt's neck. She seemed to be whispering into his ear. After a while she put a finger into the food and rubbed it on his mouth. The colt licked it off. Again Miranda dipped her finger into the food and then held it against the colt's lips. After a moment's hesitation, he cleaned off her finger. It wasn't long before he had eaten the contents of the pail. He trotted off looking less wobbly.

Miranda's eyes were shining as she climbed back over the fence with the pail.

Bill helped her over. "Nice work," he commented. "You ought to be a vet."

That's the real Miranda, thought Jennie.

They took the pail back to Pete in the stable. When they came out the door again they saw Dan Gray Wolf's ancient Ford going by on the Upper Mountain Road. Apparently Dan saw them, for he backed up and turned into the driveway. They went to meet him.

"Hi!" he called. "Want a ride home?"

Bill went over to the car and leaned his folded arms against the window frame on the driver's side. "We rode over." He nodded toward the fence where Fair Lady and Cloud were tied.

"Two horses. Three people," commented Dan.

"You can take me home," volunteered Miranda. "Then Bill can ride Fair Lady."

Bill protested. "You don't have to do that."

"Oh, I want to go home now," said Miranda. "Mrs. Mitchell is helping me make a new blouse for the picnic and I want to work on it." She pulled open the door and climbed in beside Dan.

"Picnic?" asked Dan. "What picnic?"

Bill laughed. "You must be unconscious if you haven't heard about it. The Tuscarora picnic in the grove over by the school. Hm—when is it?"

The others laughed at him.

"You know so much!" Jennie teased. "It's tomorrow

—Friday. Saturday, too. But on Friday they have the adoption ceremony, and lacrosse and fireball."

"I've never been to an Indian picnic!" Miranda was starry-eyed.

"You haven't lived yet," said Bill. "I'll buy you some corn bread. Real Indian corn bread, not that yellow stuff you whites eat."

Dan turned the key in the ignition. The motor started with a roar, but Bill continued to lean against the car. "Hold it, Dan. I have to tell you something. The state police may be paying you a visit soon." He went on to explain about Venus.

Dan listened with apparent interest, but Jennie was glad to see he didn't act worried. "Let 'em come," he said. "Long's they don't hand me a ticket for speeding they can visit me all they want to. And in this crate I can't go fast enough to bother them." He gripped the steering wheel with his broad, red-brown hands. "Tell you the truth, I can understand how a fellow might steal a horse. I'd rather have a horse than this car—or any car you can name."

"How about a Porsche like Trent's?" asked Bill.

"Well—still the horse." He looked toward the field where the colt was trotting around in his loose-jointed way. "Too bad about Venus. She was the best mare in the stable." He swung the car around and headed out of the driveway. "So long."

Jennie and Bill walked back toward their mounts. A few beginning riders were circling the paddock. How dull that must be! thought Jennie, who had ridden all her life, but never inside a ring. Her father had had a horse when he lived on the reservation and she could remember his lifting her into the saddle when she was very small. She had been under five, because she could recall her mother standing in the doorway, smiling at her daughter's pleasure. That was all she could remember of her mother, little glimpses of her—warm and loving, but never very strong. Often she was lying down, even in the daytime. Then Jennie hadn't understood, but now she knew her mother had been dying of tuberculosis. She had gone to a sanatorium, but she had waited too long before going.

Jennie glanced up at the sun and guessed that it must be nearly three o'clock.

"Grandma still believes Miranda saw a ghost horse," she told Bill, thinking how fast time was going.

Bill looked concerned. "Let's go to the lane again and look for Venus' prints. I was so burned up at Miranda this morning I gave up too soon."

"I don't think hoofprints are going to convince Grandma. She's sure Miranda's telling the truth because she gave such a good description of the ghost horse."

"Let's look for our own satisfaction," said Bill.

"All right," agreed Jennie, "but I'm afraid Fair Lady's feet have wiped out the evidence."

"Fair Lady has small feet. I wonder what kind of feet Venus has?"

Jennie saw a glimmer of hope. "Let's ask Pete!"

They looked around the field and paddock for Pete but he was not in sight.

"Maybe he's still in the stable," suggested Jennie.

He was not there, either, but just as they were about to leave, Mr. Harvey came out of his small office near the front door. Jennie gathered up her courage and approached him.

"Mr. Harvey, Bill and I have an idea. Could you tell us how big Venus' feet are?"

He stared at Jennie as if she had gone out of her mind. Then he laughed. "Oh, playing detective! I'll tell you—Venus has big feet. Better than that, I'll give you one of her old shoes. Come on."

He led the way to an empty stall and took down a horseshoe that was hanging over the entrance. "There you are. I sure hope this brings good luck to you and me, too."

"Thank you!" said Jennie. She hadn't guessed how nice Mr. Harvey was. He had always seemed quiet and stern, and she had been a little afraid of him.

Bill thrust the horseshoe through his belt as they left the stable.

"Do you want to ride Fair Lady or Cloud?" he asked.

"I'll stay with Cloud. I like him."

Bill looked pleased. "As far as money is concerned he isn't worth peanuts compared to Fair Lady. But he's a good horse, all the same."

Bill on Fair Lady led the way across the fields toward the north. At first they were on paths used by the horses from the riding stables, but then they reached a field planted with corn. Here the property of the Harvey Stables ended and the Tomilsin land began.

"How do we get through this?" asked Jennie.

"We don't. I planted this corn," said Bill, "and I don't aim to knock any of it down. I know a way around it, though."

He turned his horse to the left and continued in that direction until he reached a narrow opening where he turned right. The two horses picked their way daintily between the fields of corn.

Next they skirted a field of oats and one of wheat. Ahead lay a woodland. Jennie had never ridden across this stretch of land. As they threaded their way between the trees she was reminded of the television pictures of the winter Olympics and the way the skiers raced downhill weaving between the flags. This was like slalom on horseback.

All the way across the fields Bill and Jennie had been alert for prints of a horse's hoof or droppings, but they had seen none.

As they neared the cherry orchard, they came to a halt and tied the horses to two large maple trees with enough rope so they could graze but not become entangled with each other.

"Now we might find some prints," said Bill. The ground in the orchard had been plowed and though grass had sprung up in many places there was still much bare earth under and between the trees. "If Venus was in the lane last night she must have come across country from the stables the way we did. Let's see if we can find out where she entered the orchard."

"Funny we didn't see any tracks on the way here," worried Jennie.

"Too much ground cover," said Bill. "We could've missed them easy. Come on."

They started at the far right side of the orchard, near the Blacknose Spring Road, and walked west along the edge of the plowed ground. Jennie thought it was lucky that this area was out-of-bounds for the riding stables. Otherwise their task would have been even more hopeless.

To their disappointment they found no tracks. At the western boundary of the orchard, they turned north and walked beside the fruit-laden trees until they reached the lane. There, sure enough, were hoofprints plainly visible in the dirt, but there were many prints, one trampled upon the next.

Bill pulled the horseshoe from his belt and measured it against several prints.

"Look, isn't this hoofprint larger than this one?" he asked Jennie.

"Yes, I think so," she said doubtfully.

"I'm almost sure more than one horse has been along here recently." Bill straightened and again looped the horseshoe over his belt. "Let's follow this lane and see where the tracks take us."

CHAPTER

9

Bill and Jennie continued to walk west with the Black-nose Spring Road behind them. They kept to the side of the lane so as not to disturb any tracks.

At first the prints were many and were as jumbled as the first they had found. But looking ahead, Jennie could see that the line of hoofprints thinned out.

"They come from Kienuka!" she exclaimed.

Before them lay the plateau where the ancient Indian village now called Kienuka had stood hundreds of years before the Tuscarora came. The House of Refuge, the home of the Peace Queen, had been in this village. There fugitives from any nation had found shelter, and no killing was permitted.

"The house was named Oh-gau-strau-yea, or bark-laid-down," Jennie's grandmother had told her. "Just as people have to walk carefully on slippery elm bark, so they had to walk in the House of Refuge. It was a way of saying that they had to obey the laws of the place."

At each end of the long bark building was a door. Inside was one room, divided across the middle by a curtain. In this room the Peace Queen had kept a kettle of hominy bubbling. When a fugitive arrived, he was fed on one side of the curtain and his pursuer on the other. Then the queen talked to both, acting as a mediator. When an agreement was reached, the curtain was raised and the two enemies left in peace.

The office of the Peace Queen was a great and sacred honor, Sarah Mitchell had explained to her granddaughter. For years the queens kept their trust. But finally one queen allowed fugitives to be killed in the House of Refuge. This led to a war during which the dwellers at Kienuka were defeated. Many were adopted by their conquerors, as was the Indian custom, but the Indians who had lived at Kienuka disappeared as a nation.

In the years since then, other villages had grown up and then vanished from the ancient site, and many crops had been harvested there. Now the cabins were gone and a young orchard had been planted on the great field.

Jennie, following the trail of the hoofprints, stopped to pick up a piece of flint which was partially shaped into an arrowhead.

She showed it to Bill. "You want it?"

He shook his head. "Take it to Miranda. Might give her a thrill."

Now one set of hoofprints turned to the right, circled, and headed back toward Blacknose Spring Road. The second set of prints continued in a straight line across Kienuka.

Bill crouched to compare Venus' shoe with the second set of prints in the soft ground.

"A perfect match!" He looked triumphantly up at Jennie.

She met the gaze of Bill's brown eyes. His expression was that of one conspirator to another and she treasured the moment of closeness. "Now we know for sure Venus came through here," she said. "We may get this figured out yet."

The trail of the horse's steps crossed the young orchard, then went south on a slant to enter the western end of the same woods through which Bill and Jennie had come.

"I suppose whoever took Venus circled west to avoid the road and houses," commented Bill. "Now let's see how far we can trace her down the lane."

This was not easy, but Bill and Jennie were persistent. Soon they became expert at identifying Venus' prints among the smaller shoe marks that belonged to Fair Lady. Venus' tracks continued to show up almost to the end of the lane, but to their surprise, her steps seemed to halt about two hundred yards before the lane entered the Blacknose Spring Road.

Again and again they checked the dusty exit of the lane, but not once did they find any print the size of Venus' shoe.

Bill grinned ruefully. "Guess she did fly through the air. Miranda wasn't kidding."

Jennie walked back until she was near the small clearing she had noticed earlier. A number of cars had driven into the lane over the past few weeks, she observed, but two sets of tracks were plainer than the rest. They turned off the road to the right and disappeared into the clearing.

She paused. "Here's as far as Venus came," she said, "and none of her prints go back up the lane. She had to go *some* place. She must have been picked up by a helicopter." She looked excitedly at Bill. "Picked up! Look at those tracks!"

Bill joined her and studied the double set of tire tracks. "By a truck," he said, "or a horse trailer." He looked more closely. "Looks as if it was a trailer. See—there's a double set of tracks going in and out again." He smiled at her. "I tell you, we're a team!"

With one accord he and Jennie followed the tire marks into the clearing. Here the trail disappeared in the thick grass.

"Someone rode Venus this far," Bill guessed. "Someone with a car and trailer came here and took her away."

In the clearing a car could be well-hidden, for trees sheltered it from the lane, except for the small space where the tire tracks entered. To the north was the wooded ridge where the ground dropped sharply to the Lower Mountain Road.

Jennie began a methodical search of the clearing.

Back and forth she went, studying the ground, though already her neck ached from constant looking down. Bill followed her example, starting at the opposite end of the clearing.

"Look here!" he called.

Jennie ran to join him and saw that he had found a section where the grass was trampled and torn. Here and there a hoofprint was plainly visible.

"My guess is that Venus gave the thief a rough time," said Bill. "You know how hard it can be to get a horse into a trailer. Venus must've realized she was leaving her colt and put up a fight."

"That's when we heard her." Jennie looked toward Lake Etmejejo, and to her surprise she noticed that there were few trees in that direction. She crossed the clearing and stopped at the edge of the ridge. From there she could see over the tops of trees that grew on the slope below and could look directly across the road to the lake. "No wonder we heard her so clearly! There was nothing to stop the sound."

Bill joined her. "I'll tell the troopers about this. It may help them to know Venus was taken away in a trailer."

"Too bad we don't know where it went," said Jennie.

"Come on." Bill started down the lane. "We can find out which way it turned."

The double set of tire tracks, they discovered, went through the muddy spot at the entrance to the lane and turned south onto the Blacknose Spring Road.

"It must have gone up the road ahead of us last night,"

Jennie remarked. "Bill, I've been wondering about something. How did they get Venus to keep still? Remember, we heard the hoofbeats and that awful whinnying noise. Then all at once they stopped."

Instead of answering, Bill said, "Let's go back to the horses. We've seen everything there is to see around here." As they walked between the rows of cherry trees, he said thoughtfully, "If a barn is burning and you have to take a horse out in a hurry you put a bag over its head and it goes along with you."

"You think they did that to Venus?"

He shrugged.

Jennie felt doubtful. "It must have been some job to put a bag over Venus' head the way she was fighting."

"Yeah." Bill picked a ripe cherry and handed it to Jennie, then picked one for himself. "I don't think we ought to tell Miranda about the trailer and the clearing, or even that we found Venus' hoofprints."

"Why not?"

"The way she's been acting. You know, coming here early this morning and riding up and down the lane. Did she ever do that before?"

"No—but she said Gordon Trent wouldn't mind."

"Could be," said Bill. "But he never told me she could take Fair Lady. Looks to me as if she was trying to cover up Venus' footprints."

"I don't know why she'd do that."

"Neither do I. Except Venus' tracks knock even more holes in that ghost horse story. Anyway, no need to tell

Miranda what we found today. I have a hunch she knows more about what happened last night than we do."

Jennie hated to believe this. She said reluctantly, "I guess you're right, but Miranda wouldn't do anything wrong, like stealing a horse. We know she didn't do that because she was with us."

"Oh, I agree with you there. But something's going on and if we ever want to know the answers we have to play it smart," said Bill. "I don't think we ought to say anything to anybody—except the troopers."

The maple trees came into view and under them Cloud and Fair Lady were quietly nibbling at the grass.

"You ride Fair Lady," urged Bill. "She's great."

Jennie mounted the filly. Bill was right, Fair Lady was special. She responded intelligently to the slightest signal and picked her way over the rough ground as if she had secret knowledge of every hummock and wood-chuck hole.

As Bill rode up beside her on Cloud, Jennie asked, "Do you think there's any chance the hoofprints would make Grandma change her mind?"

"Don't tell her," said Bill. "Not yet. Word might get out to Miranda."

Jennie moaned. "We can't let Grandma tell the clan women to pick a different chief!"

"She said she'd wait till after the picnic," Bill reminded her. "The picnic's tomorrow, so we have another day to work on this. Maybe we'll find some solid evidence by then. Anything can happen."

CHAPTER
10

As Bill and Jennie came across the field behind the barn, they could see a green Porsche convertible in the driveway. The top was off and the young man behind the steering wheel was leaning back, smoking a cigarette.

"There's Gordon Trent!" said Jennie.

"Good. I want to tell him about Venus being stolen."

Jennie asked quietly, "Will you tell him about the hoofprints we found?"

Bill hesitated. "No, I guess not. And we won't even tell Mr. Harvey. Not yet, anyway. How do we know who we can trust?"

When she and Bill rounded the corner of the barn Jennie saw that Trent was not alone. Miranda was sitting beside the barn door on a weather-beaten bench, holding the cat, Eagle Eye, on her lap.

Trent lifted his head and waved a greeting.

"Hi!" called Jennie.

Bill leaped down from his horse. "I hope you haven't been waiting long, Mr. Trent. I didn't expect you."

Trent tossed away the stub of his cigarette and opened the car door. "How many times do I have to tell you to lay off with that *mister?* You make me feel like an old man." He climbed out and slammed the door behind him. Though his thinness made him seem tall, he was only of average height. "I haven't been here long," he said. "I didn't mind the wait. Miranda kept me company." He grinned at the girl on the bench.

Bill took Cloud into the barn and then came back. "Did Miranda tell you a horse is missing at the Harvey Stables?"

"Yes." Trent's narrow face was worried. "I hope Fair Lady's safe. After all, she's in a barn and near your house and Mitchells'." He seemed to be trying to reassure himself. "Wouldn't be like stealing a horse from a pasture. Still—she is a valuable horse and someone may be watching her."

"I could put a lock on the barn," Bill suggested.

"Good idea," replied Gordon. "Do you have a padlock?"

"Not on hand. Never had to lock up the barn before."

"I'll bring one out to you tomorrow." He aimed a playful punch at Miranda's arm. "And you, young lady, don't exercise my horse unless you check with Bill."

So Miranda had told him about her early morning ride! thought Jennie. That spoke well for her.

Miranda looked sulky. "I thought you said I could ride Fair Lady any time I wanted to."

"I don't mind your riding her," Gordon said. "Or Jennie, either. But let's play fair with Bill. He's in charge."

Bill said, "Thanks, Mr.—I mean, Gordon. I wouldn't like to be in the same spot as Pete Campbell. He thought Mr. Harvey's son had taken Venus and that's why he didn't report her missing."

Jennie was glad Gordon Trent had made his wishes clear on this subject. If Miranda could take Fair Lady any time she chose, Bill would never know where to find the filly.

Jennie watched Trent mount Fair Lady and start across the field behind the barn. He rode well, but not as well as Bill, she thought loyally. When Bill was in the saddle he seemed to be part of the horse.

Miranda left for the house, saying she still had work to do on her blouse. Jennie was about to follow her when Dan Gray Wolf pulled into the drive with as much of a flourish as was possible with his elderly car.

He climbed out and walked toward her and Bill in his dignified way. Whenever she saw Dan, Jennie thought of stately chiefs like Corbett Sundown of the Seneca Band, Cornelius Seneca, the President of the Seneca Nation, and Clinton Rickard, the great Tuscarora leader.

Dan was smiling broadly.

"Seen any ghost horses lately?" he asked.

Bill and Jennie looked at each other in dismay. If word about a ghost horse got around, Uncle Fred might lose his chance to become a chief whether Grandma said anything to the women of the clan or not.

"Did Miranda tell you?" asked Bill.

Dan nodded.

So that was why Miranda wanted to ride home with Dan today! thought Jennie. And she had promised not to mention the ghost horse to anyone. Bill was right. Miranda could not be trusted. At every evidence of Miranda's faithlessness, Jennie was more disappointed. She *liked* Miranda and they had had such good times together. She wanted to believe in her.

Tired from a day of worry and searching for clues, Jennie went to bed early. Sometime in the night she awakened suddenly from a sound sleep. She sat up, trying to recall what had aroused her. Somewhere in her drowsy mind, the memory was stored.

Out in the barn a horse whinnied. That was it! It was unusual for the horses to whinny at night. Something or someone must have disturbed them.

Quietly she went to the window. The moon, which was just about to set, shed a soft light on the field, but though she gazed intently at the barn she could not see anything or anyone moving.

The whinny had sounded like a greeting. Perhaps Bill had gone out to check on the horses. Jennie waited, but no more sounds came from the barn and still no shadow moved. What had unsettled the horses? What if the same person who took Venus was after Fair Lady?

She thought of phoning the police, but she didn't like to call them on such a slight suspicion of trouble. They would be annoyed if they arrived to find no one there or to discover only Bill Tomilsin in the barn, checking on the horses.

Of course she could phone Bill, but that would wake up everyone in his house.

Plainly it was up to her to go out to the barn to see for herself. If someone was out there saddling Fair Lady, she would never forgive herself.

With her heart thumping heavily, Jennie put on her sneakers and robe. She was much more uneasy than she had been the night before when she had gone out to look for Miranda, for now she knew that a thief had been in the area.

The thought of Miranda made her turn to the bed across the room. Something about it didn't look right. Jennie drew closer and put her hand on the rumpled blankets. Miranda was not in bed.

Jennie fumbled in the dark for the extra flashlight she kept in her top dresser drawer. Then, careful to avoid squeaky boards, she went downstairs and let herself out the back door.

The cool night air bore a refreshing scent of earth and grass and Grandma's carnations all combined. Without switching on her flashlight she hurried toward the barn. After only a few steps the dew had soaked through the canvas of her sneakers, chilling her feet. As she crossed the field, her pajama legs were soon wet from the weeds.

She was now near enough to see that the barn door was ajar. Should she turn on the flashlight? she wondered. She didn't want to frighten Miranda if she were inside the barn. On the other hand, if it were an intruder . . .

Stealthy footsteps rattled the gravel of the driveway. Jennie froze. The steps came on.

A familiar voice asked gruffly, "Who's there?"

Recognizing Bill's voice, Jennie let out the breath she had been holding.

"It's me, Jennie!" she whispered. As Bill came closer, she added, "I think Miranda's in the barn. She isn't in her bed."

"Do you have a light?"

For answer, Jennie thrust her flashlight into his hands. She seemed always to be supplying him with a light. He probably had come out in too much of a hurry to think of bringing one himself.

Bill threw the door open wide and at the same time turned on the flashlight.

Jennie heard a startled cry. Sure enough, in the beam of light stood Miranda.

CHAPTER

11

Bill and Jennie stared at Miranda.

"What are you doing here?" demanded Bill.

Miranda blinked in the glare of the flashlight and put her hand up to her eyes in a childish gesture that was appealing. "I—I wanted to be sure Fair Lady was safe. I woke up and thought I heard someone in the drive."

Bill lowered the flashlight. "*Was* anyone here?"

"No."

Bill gave a sigh of exasperation. "You'd better be glad you didn't surprise a horse thief. Don't you realize that was a dangerous thing to do?"

"I know. I was scared." Miranda kept her eyes on the floor of the barn.

Last night and now again tonight she had gone out alone. Why didn't she ask me to go with her? Jennie wondered. For a girl who was afraid of the dark, Miranda certainly acted strangely. Yet, to be fair, Jennie felt she must defend Miranda.

"Bill, I did the same thing she did. I heard a whinny and I came out to investigate. We have Fair Lady on our minds and we don't want anything to happen to her."

"You're both crazy!" Bill exclaimed. "Boy, I'm sure glad Gordon is bringing a padlock tomorrow so we can all get some sleep!"

Bill checked on the horses, and then led the girls out of the barn and closed the door.

To Jennie's surprise Miranda began to giggle. "Look who just came out of the barn!" She sounded as if she were halfway between laughter and tears as she bent to pick up Eagle Eye, the cat.

Jennie exclaimed, "So that's our horse thief!" But she knew it was not the cat that Miranda had heard in the driveway. His velvety paws never made a sound.

Bill did not seem amused. He pulled the cord of his plaid flannel robe tighter with an angry yank. "Go to bed!" He stalked across the grass to his house.

Jennie and Miranda went quietly up to their bedroom. No sound came from Grandpa and Grandma Mitchell's room. They must have slept through it all, Jennie thought gratefully.

"Do you think Bill is really mad at us?" whispered Miranda.

Jennie thought it over. "I don't believe he is. I think he acted cross because we might have been in danger."

The next morning Jennie awakened early to feel Miranda shaking her and saying, "Look! A beautiful day for the picnic." She pointed to the window where already the sun was gilding the sill and a breeze was stirring the white curtains.

Miranda raced through breakfast. "I still haven't finished my blouse," she said, "and I *have* to wear it."

Jennie knew how she felt. "I'll help you," she offered.

"Thanks, but I want to be able to say I did it all myself," said Miranda.

Grandma was too quiet and Jennie was afraid she was worrying about the ghost horse.

"You won't say anything today to the women about choosing a new chief, will you?" Jennie begged. "One more day won't do any harm."

"No, I won't spoil the picnic for them," said Grandma, "and I hope you're right that we're safe in waiting." Still, she didn't look happy.

Jennie wished she could tell her about finding Venus' footprints in the lane, but she had promised not to mention that. Bill was right, they had to keep quiet about their discovery until they were sure whom they could trust.

After breakfast she practiced the piano for a few minutes but she soon gave up as she couldn't keep her mind on scales.

She was vacuuming the living room rug when Bill burst into the room, shouting over the noise of the cleaner. He was more excited than she had ever seen him.

She turned off the switch. "I couldn't hear a word," she said. "What did you say?"

"The saddle!" he cried, pointing toward the barn. "Fair Lady's saddle is gone!"

"Are you sure?"

"Of course I'm sure. It isn't hanging on the wall and I looked all over the barn and outside, too."

Miranda came in from the kitchen, carrying her sewing with her. "You wouldn't believe me. I told you I heard someone outside last night! I bet they took the saddle."

"I suppose so." Bill looked dejected. "But that doesn't help me any. Gordon was crazy about that saddle. He may move Fair Lady out of my barn."

Jennie said heatedly, "You couldn't help it! Come on, let's all look for it and then if we don't find it, let's call the troopers."

She led the way to the barn, hoping that Bill had been wrong and that she would see the beautiful silver-trimmed saddle hanging in its accustomed spot on the south wall. But at a glance she could see that Bill was right. Cloud's saddle was on the wall and so, apparently, was all of the other tack—but not Fair Lady's saddle.

Jennie examined the remaining equipment more closely. "The saddle pad is gone, too," she told Bill. It had been a thick pad, the best she had ever seen.

Dan Gray Wolf pulled into the drive as Jennie, Bill, and Miranda came out of the barn. He was dressed in his paint-spattered working clothes.

"Hey, you going to work?" asked Bill.

"Yeah," Dan said gloomily. "I was called in. A couple

of fellows are off sick. I almost turned them down, but I'll get time-and-a-half and I can use the money." He opened the rear door of the car. "You looking for something? Maybe I have it here."

To Jennie's astonishment Dan reached into the back seat of his car and pulled out a fleece-lined saddle pad.

"That's Fair Lady's, isn't it?" he asked, tossing it to Bill.

"You're right!" Bill caught the pad and turned it over, examining it carefully. "No doubt about it. Where'd you get it?"

"I found it in my car this morning."

"You didn't find a saddle with it, did you?" asked Bill. "That's missing, too."

It was Dan's turn to look surprised. "How come?"

"We think it was taken last night," said Bill. "Miranda heard a noise and came out to investigate. She didn't see anyone, though."

"Maybe she scared them away," suggested Dan.

Bill nodded. "Yeah. Someone could've planned to take Fair Lady, but when he heard Miranda, he grabbed what he could and took off."

Dan slammed the rear door of his car. "And the skunk tossed the saddle pad in my car, trying to pin the blame on me. That's what it looks like." He slid into the front seat. "I've got to go. I'm supposed to be at work."

"What about the picnic?" asked Bill. "When will you get off work?"

"I don't know. We'll probably paint as long as it's

light. Have to take advantage of the good weather. I'll come to the picnic when I get through. I'll look you up."

"You can eat at the picnic," Jennie told him. "I'll save something for you if you want me to. Grandma and I always help at the food table."

"Thanks, do that," said Dan.

As Dan drove away, Miranda asked, "Are you going to tell the troopers about the saddle pad being in Dan's car?"

"I ought to," Bill said. "It's evidence."

"And in a way it helps clear Dan," Jennie suggested. "If he were guilty, he wouldn't have brought the pad to you. Unless—" An idea had come unbidden to her mind. Dan might have said the pad was placed in his car just because he thought it would turn suspicion away from him. She tried to thrust the unwanted thought from her mind.

Bill met her eyes. "I know what you're thinking," he said. "But I trust Dan. I know he's OK. Besides," he said with a laugh, "he doesn't even have a horse." Then he sobered and walked back toward the barn with the saddle pad. "I know," he said. "He wouldn't have to own a horse to steal a saddle. It's a valuable saddle and Dan needs money." Bill turned a troubled face toward Jennie. "But he wouldn't get it that way. I know he wouldn't."

CHAPTER
12

Miranda was working feverishly on her blouse and Jennie was making cherry pies for the picnic when Gordon Trent arrived.

Through the kitchen window Jennie saw the green Porsche stop in front of the barn. Trent got out and talked with Bill, then both disappeared into the barn. A few minutes later Trent drove away.

Curious though she was, Jennie continued to roll pie crust and to mix sugar and flour and a dash of almond extract into the cherry filling. It's none of my business what Gordon Trent says, she told herself, but she was glad when Bill leaped up the back steps and joined her in the kitchen.

"He was swell," were Bill's first words. "He said he couldn't blame me for the loss of the saddle, and anyway it was insured. He just hopes the insurance holds when the barn wasn't locked."

"Did he bring you a padlock?" asked Jennie.

"Yes. And he gave me a key and kept one for himself." Bill fished in his pocket and pulled out a key which he held up.

"Good," said Jennie. "Now the horses will be safe."

"I feel a lot better about them," said Bill. "I wouldn't dare leave today if I couldn't lock the barn."

"I wonder if the police are still looking for Venus." Jennie dropped her voice in case Miranda or Grandma was within earshot. "Did you phone the troopers about the tracks in the lane?"

"Yes. You don't think I'd forget that, do you?" Bill helped himself to a pitted cherry from the bowl. As he ate it he made a face. "Ugh! That's sour."

"Serves you right. I haven't put sugar on those yet."

Bill licked off his fingers. "Say, how about going to the picnic with me? You and Miranda. I'll pick you up at one o'clock."

"Great!" said Jennie. "Oh, we won't be able to come home with you, though. Cousin Tessie is having the usual family party after the picnic." Jennie wished Cousin Tessie didn't always feel she had to celebrate Grandpa and Grandma's wedding anniversary on the night of the picnic. It was too much for one day, but Tessie said it was the only time she could get the whole family together.

"That's OK," said Bill. "And I'll have to come home before supper time to feed the horses and pick up my father and mother. They're just going for the night program."

Going to the picnic with Bill was practically a date, thought Jennie as she dressed with special care, choosing her brown slacks to wear with her yellow blouse. She parted her hair in the middle and tied each side with a yellow ribbon.

She was quite satisfied with her own appearance until she saw Miranda in her new blouse. It was a violet shade of blue that matched her eyes to perfection and brought out the pink and white beauty of her skin.

"You look great!" Jennie told her with sincere admiration.

"So do you!" exclaimed Miranda.

As they ran downstairs together, Jennie thought warmly that Miranda was just like a sister. For the moment their differences over the ghost horse were forgotten.

"You look lovely," Grandma told them. "Have a good time. And remember, we leave for Cousin Tessie's at ten. That ought to give you a chance to see part of the fireball game. Don't make me have to look for you."

When Bill drove up to the back door in his parents' car, Miranda and Jennie carried out the pies and set them on the floor behind the front seat.

Bill looked admiringly at the two girls. "Wow! How lucky can a guy be?"

Miranda leaped into the front seat and slid over to the middle. Jennie had thought she would sit next to Bill, but she told herself that Miranda, being smaller, probably thought she would fit better in the middle.

The picnic grounds were only a mile from the house, near the Tuscarora school where Jennie had attended kindergarten through fourth grade. From the fourth grade on, she and the other Tuscaroras went to the big central school not far away where they mingled with the non-Indian students from the countryside to the east of the city of Niagara Falls.

Only a playing field lay between the school and the picnic grove. In that field the boys would play lacrosse today, and later that night, fireball.

Bill parked the car beside the road and the three walked leisurely into the grove of pine and maple where the booths were already in place. Fringed crepe paper fluttered from the ridge poles, and colorful beaded costumes on many of the Indian men and women added to the festive atmosphere.

Jennie looked around happily. The annual picnic was a familiar but always fascinating experience. This was a beautiful day and she wasn't going to worry about a ghost horse or anything.

Suddenly she found that she was alone. Miranda had seized Bill's arm and was pulling him toward the first booth where an Indian was demonstrating how to make lacrosse sticks.

Jennie followed them. Miranda wanted to buy a stick, but Bill talked her out of it.

"It's a rough game," he told her. "You'll see when we play this afternoon. It's no sport for a girl."

Miranda pouted. "All right, but I want to buy something. I have plenty of money."

"Lucky you," said Bill.

Miranda said defensively, "My stepfather left it to me."

They wandered on past the hamburger and hot dog stands and lingered at one shaped like a tepee where Indian crafts were sold. Here Miranda bought two pairs of beaded earrings, blue to match her blouse and yellow to go with Jennie's. Then she insisted on buying a bolo tie for Bill. In spite of his protests she slid the loop of leather over his head and adjusted the beaded slide that bore a thunderbird design.

Jennie could not help feeling annoyed at the way Miranda was taking possession of Bill, but she was determined not to show her feelings by word or expression. This, too, had been part of her training.

"There, Bill, you look beautiful!" said Miranda with a satisfied air.

Bill shrugged self-consciously and looked at Jennie. *Beautiful* wasn't quite the word to describe him, she thought. But he was handsome with his face a little redder than usual and the amused look in his steady brown eyes.

Miranda wanted to see everything. When the breeze brought them the scent of corn soup, she headed for the huge iron pot. On tiptoes she peered at the thick, bubbling mixture that was being stirred by an Indian woman dressed in a gathered cotton skirt and beaded blouse.

A moment later she was hurrying toward the archery range and Bill was following obediently. They stood on the sidelines watching as the marksmen took careful aim before sending the arrows swishing through the air to plunge quivering into the target. Some of the archers were in Indian costume.

Miranda stood beside Bill, talking to him and smiling up at him with her violet eyes.

The sun was warm on Jennie's head and in the distance the band played. A woman with a beautiful, clear voice sang "The Indian Love Call." Everything was the same as usual—yet different. Other years she had come to the picnic for the games and good things to eat. Now she was old enough to suffer over a boy she liked. She fingered one of the yellow earrings that she wore and wished she could feel grateful for them. She knew she would never enjoy wearing them for they would always remind her of this day.

"Adoption ceremony in five minutes!" blared the loud-speaker.

This time it was Bill who made the decision. "Let's go," he said. "We have to see that."

The benches, arranged in a semi-circle in front of the platform, were beginning to fill up. It was a holiday-minded audience of Indians from other reservations as well as Tuscaroras and non-Indians from miles around.

Bill found seats in front of the stage where a chief in bead-decorated red shirt and trousers was introducing the two Seneca Indians who were in charge of the adoption ceremony. Every step of the ritual was familiar to Bill and Jennie. Miranda, again seated between them, kept up a barrage of questions.

A distinguished-looking United States Senator was being adopted into the Tuscarora nation because he had shown concern for the Indians' problems. The two Senecas danced and sang and led the senator to the four corners of the stage in each of which an Indian stood.

"Why do they do that?" asked Miranda.

"The corners of the platform stand for the four corners of the earth," said Bill, "and the leader is asking if the senator should be accepted into the tribe."

A moment later Miranda whispered, "Why do the Senecas take charge of the adoption?"

"Those men know the ritual so they go to other reservations to do adoptions," answered Jennie. "The Senecas are special to us, though. They gave us some of the land we live on now."

"Your ancestors drove us out of North Carolina more than two hundred years ago," Bill told Miranda. "That's why we had to find a new home. Just lucky for us the Five Nations of the Iroquois took us in. We made it Six Nations."

Miranda frowned at him. "Don't blame me. I wasn't even born then, and if I had been I wouldn't have driven you out."

"Maybe you wouldn't, but the white men are still

pushing us. We lost a lot of land to the Niagara Power Project just a few years ago."

Miranda said indignantly, "They paid you!"

Bill shrugged. "What's money? In a few years that's gone. Land lasts forever. That's what we Indians want —our own land where we can live the way we want to."

One of the Tuscarora chiefs brought the ceremony to a climax by the placing of a huge feathered headdress on the senator's head.

Bill muttered, "They shouldn't have that kind of headdress. That's not Tuscarora."

"Why not use it?" asked Miranda. "It's pretty."

"The Tuscaroras were woodland Indians," Jennie explained. "A feathered headdress like that would have gotten caught in the trees. That kind was used by the western Indians who lived in open country."

"This feathered job makes a bigger impression on you whites than the headband and two or three feathers the Tuscaroras used to wear," added Bill teasingly.

Two women came down the aisle at the far right side of the audience. Jennie's attention was caught by the movement, and as she glanced at the newcomers she stiffened with surprise. She nudged Miranda.

"Isn't that Miss Hugo?" she asked.

"Where?"

"Over there, in the third row from the front."

Miranda looked quickly and then turned away. "It doesn't look like her to me."

"I'm sure that's who it is," said Jennie. She started to

rise. "Miranda, I—I'm going to ask her about the ghost horse."

Miranda pulled her down. "I don't care what you ask her, but you can't go now. *He's* going to make a speech."

It was true. The senator was at the microphone and it would be impolite to leave.

"My friends, brothers and sisters of the Tuscarora . . ." he began. To Jennie the speech seemed endless. All during it she kept her eyes on Miss Hugo. Inside that head with its neat brown hair might be the answer to the riddle of the ghost horse.

At last the senator sat down, but to Jennie's dismay Miss Hugo left her seat and walked quickly toward the rear of the audience.

Jennie jumped to her feet with a hasty, "See you later," and worked her way into the crowd already filling the aisle.

Behind her she heard Bill say to Miranda, "Time for lacrosse. Come and watch me play."

Miss Hugo was small and Jennie found it difficult to keep her in sight. Apparently she was headed for the road, so Jennie inched her way in that direction, hoping to intercept her.

Every now and then some friend or relative tried to stop Jennie as she wove in and out of the throng. After she passed the handicraft tepee and the lacrosse booth she emerged into the open where she could make more speed. Unfortunately, Miss Hugo, also, was moving faster. She was fumbling in her purse as she walked, probably searching for her car keys, Jennie thought.

She called, "Miss Hugo!" but her shout was lost in the noise of traffic and the music of the band that was again playing.

CHAPTER

13

Miss Hugo came to a halt at a tan Volkswagen. She was inside and the door was closed before Jennie, breathless and all but speechless, reached her.

Clinging to the door handle, Jennie panted, "Miss Hugo! I have—to ask you—a question!"

Miss Hugo looked up with concern in her pale blue eyes. "Why, Jennie, whatever's the matter?" She glanced at her watch. "I'm late for an appointment in Buffalo, but go ahead."

Briefly Jennie told the events of the past few days and then asked, "Did you ever tell Miranda about the ghost horse that looked like a skeleton with a big head?"

Miss Hugo answered emphatically, "I've never in my life heard a story about a ghost horse. I couldn't have told it to Miranda."

Despairingly Jennie watched the car drive away. There went her best hope for proving that Miranda had made up the story of the ghost horse. Of course she could tell Grandma of finding Venus' hoofprints in the lane and of the tire tracks that entered the clearing, but she had little hope that those bits of evidence would convince Grandma. It would take more than that to make her doubt Miranda's word.

Jennie started toward the lacrosse field, but on the way she saw her grandmother beckoning to her. Grandma looked every inch the clan mother in a brown dress with a fringed hem. As a crowning touch she wore a beaded headband with a feather standing proudly erect in back.

"I was looking for you, Jennie," she said. "We could use your help with the serving."

Jennie began to object. She wanted to watch Bill play lacrosse and she didn't want to leave him alone with Miranda, but her protest died in her throat. Helping with the food was her job. Grandma, taking it for granted that she would follow, was trotting back toward the food tables. In spite of her jaunty air, Jennie knew she must be tired, for she had been up since early that morning, baking for the picnic.

After a detour to tell Miranda where she would be, Jennie went to work, warmed by Bill's friendly wave from the playing field. Even in the midst of the game he had noticed her.

All the rest of the afternoon Jennie put scoops of potato salad and baked beans on an endless line of paper plates, only taking time out to eat with Bill and Miranda. The time passed more quickly than she had expected.

Friends greeted her as they went through the line. Her relatives and some of the older people made little jokes and teased her.

"You Indians are always laughing about something," Miranda had remarked one day. "It's like you were one big family."

It was partly true, thought Jennie. What Miranda didn't understand was that Indians often laughed to hide their unhappiness with their lot. They didn't want the white man's world of money and possessions, and yet they couldn't return to their forefathers' way of life. They were lost between two worlds.

Miranda was right, though, about the Tuscaroras being like a family. Oh, they had their differences, but if one of them needed help—got sick or had a fire—everyone on the reservation was ready to help. What would it be like to be an outsider here? she wondered. Miranda must often feel lonely.

Remembering her promise to Dan Gray Wolf, Jennie put aside a heaping plate of food for him, but when he didn't appear, finally she gave it to one of the small boys who was hanging around the food table with a hungry look in his brown eyes.

It was almost dark before Jennie was free to join the people who were gathering along the edge of the field to watch the fireball game. She sank gratefully onto the grass beside Bill and Miranda.

The goal posts, wrapped in kerosene-soaked rags,

were in place. The coach brought out the ball made of tightly wrapped rags and twine. It, too, had been dipped in kerosene. One of the men touched the rags on the goal posts with a torch and then set the ball on fire.

The game began. It was soccer with a burning ball. In the darkness it was eerie to see a kick shoot the ball of flame into the air. As soon as it touched the ground another foot was always ready to send it forward or backward. The players leaped agilely this way and that to avoid being struck by the ball.

Suddenly the ball soared out of the field toward the watching crowd. People screamed and scrambled out of its path. No one was injured, but the grass caught fire.

Immediately boys came running with the pails of water that were kept ready for such an emergency. As soon as the grass fire was out, the teams again grouped on the field, but now one of the goal posts had burned through and collapsed.

Jennie heard someone say, "Jennie? That you?"

It was Grandpa Mitchell.

"Yes, Grandpa. What is it?"

"It's time to go to Tessie's. Your grandma's in the car now."

Jennie got wearily to her feet. "All right. Ready, Miranda?"

"Oh, no! I want to see the rest of the game!" cried Miranda.

"Sorry," said Grandpa. "They can't play without that goal post and it'll take some time to get that fixed. Grandma and I are the guests of honor, so we mustn't be late."

"Please, Mr. Mitchell, let me stay," Miranda pleaded. "Bill will bring me home, won't you, Bill?"

Jennie saw Bill's head turn in her direction. Then he replied, "Sure, I'll take Miranda home if it's all right with you, Mr. Mitchell."

Jennie was about to say, "I'd like to stay, too," but then she saw that Miranda was clinging to Bill's arm. Her blonde head shone gold next to Bill's shoulder. He didn't have to let her hang onto him like that, did he? It must be he liked it.

"Let's go, Grandpa," said Jennie abruptly.

Bill stood up. "See you tomorrow, Jennie."

Jennie managed to respond, "Right. Good night." Then without a backward glance she followed her grandfather to the car. She couldn't bear to look again at those two sitting close together side by side. Probably they were glad she had gone. Bill had said he liked her Indian look but apparently he admired blonde girls even more.

Why shouldn't he like Miranda better than me? she asked herself. She's prettier than I am. And I don't have any claim on him. We're just friends. But her heart felt like lead.

As Grandpa started the car she realized how weary

she was. She didn't see how she could stand another two or three hours of talk and serving and eating more food.

"I'm awfully tired," she said. "Would you mind dropping me off at the house?"

Grandma objected, but Grandpa seemed to understand. "She's had a hard day," he said. "She can go home if she wants to."

When Grandpa made up his mind even Grandma knew it was no use to try to change it.

Jennie let herself into the empty house and her grandparents drove away.

It felt good to be home and to be alone. She felt like an injured animal that crawls to its den to lick its wounds. She kept wondering, when Miranda knew how she felt about Bill, how could she make up to him? That wasn't the way a friend should act.

Dropping her purse onto a chair, Jennie went to the piano. It rarely failed to comfort her, but tonight it didn't help. She played a final crashing chord and gave up.

What had happened to Dan Gray Wolf? she wondered. He had missed the entire picnic.

Listlessly she wandered to the kitchen where the service light on the back of the electric stove sent a dim glow throughout the room. The baked beans and potato salad had made her thirsty and she poured herself a glass of water from the bottle in the refrigerator.

Glass in hand, she went to the window. The yard had

a silvery look and the weathered boards of the barn were almost white in the moonlight.

Something about the barn kept her eyes riveted to it. A black space gaped in the front where the door should have been. The barn door was open!

CHAPTER

14

The barn door shouldn't be open now! thought Jennie. Bill had come home late that afternoon to feed the horses. She had seen him leave with Miranda shortly after the lacrosse game. Could he have been in such a hurry he had forgotten to close and lock the door? That wasn't like Bill.

She started out the back door, then returned for her flashlight. The moon had disappeared behind a cloud. As she hurried across the field, she mused that visiting the barn by night was getting to be a habit with her. And with Miranda, she thought.

What *was* the matter with Miranda? She had developed a Dr. Jekyll and Mr. Hyde personality, pleasant and lovable one minute, distant and mysterious the next.

Yes, the barn door was wide open, Jennie discovered as she drew nearer. But something about it was strange. It was standing open the wrong way. How could a door open on the side where the hinges were?

Now she was near enough to examine it closely. The padlock was still firmly in place. Someone had removed the hinges from the door!

Her puzzlement gave way to dread and she backed away. The person who had taken off the hinges might still be here. For two or three minutes she waited, straining her ears for sounds inside the barn.

Finally she called out, "Who's there?"

The sound of her own voice startled her, but there was no answer.

Snapping on her flashlight, she advanced to the open doorway. Her worst fears were realized. Cloud stood quietly in his stall, but Fair Lady was missing.

Jennie beamed her light around the barn to be sure the horse was not standing in an unnoticed corner. It would be difficult, she thought with bitter humor, to hide so large a creature.

Whirling around, she ran back to the house. Someone had stolen Fair Lady, she was sure. This time Miranda was not out riding for she and Bill were still at the picnic. Gordon hadn't taken his filly, as he had a key to the barn. If he had had a sudden desire to ride his horse, he'd have unlocked the door.

Someone had stolen Fair Lady, thought Jennie—probably the same person who had taken Venus.

Wasting no more time, she ran back to the house and called the state police. When she had given her information to the trooper who answered the phone, she added, "Maybe the thief went to that lane Bill Tomilsin told you about, and you can catch him there. You know, the place where we found Venus' hoofprints."

"We can't spare anyone right now," the trooper said in his businesslike way. "There's been a bad accident at Military and Packard Roads and every car is out. I'll send a call for them to check on the horse as soon as they can but people come first, you know."

Jennie hung up and wondered what she should do next. By the time the troopers were free to come, Fair Lady might be so far away they never would find her.

She wondered if Gordon Trent would blame Bill for the loss of his horse. At any rate, Bill wouldn't have his well-paying job and he'd never forgive himself for Fair Lady's disappearance. He loved that filly and he'd feel terrible.

For Bill's sake, as well as the filly's, Jennie decided she must do what she could to find out where Fair Lady had gone. The most likely place to look was the clearing beside the lane.

Jennie ran out the back door and again sprinted across the field to the barn, the flashlight in her hand bobbing up and down, throwing its light first on the ground and then into the sky.

In the barn she stopped only long enough to put on Cloud's bridle. If she hesitated a moment she was afraid she might not go ahead with her plan. She could just hear Grandma saying she should let the police take care of thieves. But she knew she would never forgive herself if she remained at home while someone made off with Fair Lady.

With her heart racing, she led the sturdy pinto outside and, using the bench beside the door as a step, flung herself onto his back. Still pushing aside her doubts, she urged the horse down the drive. She would have to follow the Blacknose Spring Road to the lane as she wouldn't take the chance of having Cloud fall and break a leg in the field or woods. Besides, she felt she would be safer on the road than in the deserted fields.

At the road she turned north, keeping the horse on the shoulder, which in the reservation was grassy. She would have to approach the lane quietly if she were to catch the thief by surprise. What she would do if she did find him, she didn't know. She hoped she could watch from a hiding place and discover which way he went so she could tell the police when they arrived.

Cloud stumbled over a large stone but recovered himself quickly.

"Easy," Jennie whispered. In spite of her fear and worry, she felt a wild pleasure in the ride through the darkness. It had been at least a year since she had ridden bareback, but when she was younger she had rarely used a saddle.

A car sped by, then slowed down after it had passed her. No doubt the driver was wondering why a horse and rider were out so late. However, the car didn't stop and again Jennie was alone. She wondered if the driver of the car might be a friend of the thief who would report her approach. Well, if he did, he did, she thought.

In the stillness the thud of Cloud's hoofs on the sod seemed to fill the night. If the thief has ears he'll hear me coming, thought Jennie, but if he's riding Fair Lady he may not hear other hoofbeats.

The fireball game must be over by now. She wondered if Bill and Miranda would go home or to Cousin Tessie's. Or would they go someplace for a coke or hot dog? This idea gave her such a jealous pang she pushed it from her mind.

Anyway, she thought, whenever Bill came home he'd discover that Fair Lady was missing. Perhaps he, too, would think of going to the lane.

I should have left a note, realized Jennie, so he'd know I took Cloud. But she hadn't had time for note-writing.

The thief had chosen an ideal time. It was one of the few nights during the year when everyone would be away from home. It could not have been chance. The person or persons who took Fair Lady must have known the reservation well. It might even be someone she knew —probably the same person who stole Venus.

Pete Campbell had told the troopers that Dan Gray Wolf was always hanging around the Harvey Stables. Dan had not come to the picnic as he had said he would. Had he really been called to work today? She was sure he wasn't painting the bridge after dark.

Just ahead on her left was the grove of trees where Uncle Fred's home was located. The porch light shone among the trees in front of the house, sending long shadows onto the grass. No one was home yet. Uncle Fred and all of his family were at Cousin Tessie's party.

The lane was near at hand and Jennie was increasingly conscious of the noise of Cloud's hoofs. She would have to leave him some place and go the rest of the way on foot. After considering the garage as a temporary stable, she gave up the idea when she pictured her uncle whipping into the driveway and coming to a halt with squealing brakes at the sight of a horse in his garage. Cloud might be startled enough to rear up and be injured.

Turning onto the driveway she then circled behind the house until she reached a sheltered area she knew. Here a dip in the ground made a hollow that was surrounded by pine and hemlock trees and honeysuckle bushes. It was ideal for a hiding place.

As she maneuvered Cloud between the trees, one of her yellow hair ribbons caught on a branch. She reached for it too late as it slipped off and disappeared into the shadows. No matter, she thought, tucking her hair behind her ear, she'd find it tomorrow by daylight.

She tied Cloud to a sturdy pine and, with a reassuring pat, left him. On foot she returned to the road and padded along the verge toward the lane. When a car approached, she dived behind a tree and watched, hoping to see a police car. It was a station wagon, however, that roared by and continued down the hill past Lake Etmejejo to the Lower Mountain Road.

When she reached the entrance to the lane she longed to check for hoofprints or tire marks, but she didn't dare turn on the flashlight she had tucked into her jacket pocket. The light might carry too far and warn the thief of her approach.

For several minutes she stood in the shadows beside the lane with her head lifted, listening for any sound that might tell her whether or not Fair Lady and the unknown thief were near at hand. A fresh breeze from the lake ruffled her hair and cooled her face. From a nearby tree a mourning dove called and, far to her left, perhaps as far away as Kienuka, she heard what she thought was the boom of a partridge. In vain she waited to hear the stamp or whinny of a horse or the purr of a motor.

The silence and darkness quelled some of Jennie's spirit of adventure. As familiar as she was with this area, she didn't want to go down the lane tonight. She looked up the road, longing for the approach of a police car, but no car of any kind came. In the darkness, even the specks of light from the fireflies were welcome.

Perhaps she should wait here until the troopers came, but they might not arrive for an hour or more. At last curiosity drew her up the lane, as well as her desire to save Fair Lady and to prove to Grandma that there was no ghost horse. If she could hide at the edge of the clearing where the thief and filly must be she might see or hear something that would solve the entire mystery. By staying out of sight of the thief she should be safe.

She turned to the left, and, with one hand before her face to ward off unseen branches, she began to work her way through the weeds and brushy trees to the cherry orchard. The lane was only a few feet to her right. Soon the plowed ground of the orchard was under her feet and she felt the cool touch of cherries against her hand. Birds, disturbed by her coming, rose from the trees with a rustle of leaves and wings.

Be quiet! she wanted to say.

As soon as she judged she had come almost as far as the clearing, she turned right. At the lane she stopped to look and listen, but she could see little in the dim light and could hear no sound that was not native to the night.

At last she crossed the lane and felt her way to the entrance of the clearing where she and Bill had seen evidence of a struggle. When she reached it, she paused again before she stepped inside. The clearing was empty.

Jennie's heart sank. The thief must have come and gone. By now Fair Lady was far away.

As she returned to the lane, she dared to snap on her light to examine the ground. To her disappointment she found no fresh car tracks entering the clearing. The thief must have gone to a different place to meet the car and trailer this time. Perhaps he had driven directly to the barn, since tonight neither the Mitchells nor the Tomilsins had been home. Of course, he must have backed the trailer up to the barn and loaded Fair Lady right there. Why hadn't she thought of that?

Downcast, she started toward Blacknose Spring Road and came to an abrupt halt after only a few paces. In the glow from her flashlight fresh tire tracks were plain in the dirt. Jennie turned around, keeping her light on the tracks. They continued up the lane past the clearing.

Probably they were the tracks of a car containing a pair of lovers who wanted to be alone, but they might have been made by a truck or van that had come for Fair Lady.

CHAPTER

15

As Jennie walked cautiously up the road, she turned off her flashlight and left it off except for occasional quick flicks of the switch to be sure the tracks were continuing. On and on they went and still she found no car.

Though her hands felt clammy with excitement, she didn't actually expect to find Fair Lady or the thief this far up the lane. The new little orchard that was planted on the site of Kienuka was not far ahead. She skirted a muddy patch where the lane was well-sheltered by large trees, rounded a bend, and almost walked directly into a strange scene.

Cautiously she drew back and edged her way among the trees on her left. Then, crouched behind a bush, she peered through the leafy branches.

In the circle of light from an electric lantern which was standing on the ground, were a man and a horse. The horse was Fair Lady. Jennie knew she would recognize that fine, proud head anywhere. The man was crouched beside the horse, doing something to her feet. When he finished with one foot he moved on to another. Soon Jennie realized he was dyeing Fair Lady's white socks!

A car was parked beyond the man and horse, but in the darkness Jennie could not even tell its color. It must be the car whose tracks she had followed.

So far she had not been able to see the man clearly, either, but as he moved to work on another foot, the lantern light shone full on his face. With a shock she saw that the man was Gordon Trent, the owner of Fair Lady!

He couldn't steal his own horse! Why was he dyeing her socks? And why had he removed the hinges from the barn door instead of unlocking the padlock?

No longer afraid, Jennie was on the verge of stepping from the cover of the bush and asking Mr. Trent what he was doing. But just as she stood up, she heard the sound of a motor not far away. A car was coming down the lane.

Jennie settled back behind the bush and decided to wait before making her presence known.

As the car came closer Trent heard it, too, and stood up, looking anxiously in the direction of the sound. Fair Lady moved restlessly. Jennie guessed that the filly was nervous over these unfamiliar happenings.

The car rounded the bend in the lane and came into view. Only it was not a car, but a pickup truck pulling a one-horse trailer. The driver went past, then backed the trailer into the open land between Gordon Trent and the place where Jennie was hiding.

Although the rear of the trailer was only a few feet away, by shifting slightly, Jennie still had a good view of Trent and Fair Lady. Silently she watched the driver saunter across the clearing.

He looked familiar, but Jennie couldn't place him. Where had she seen that walk before?

Trent called out softly, "Where have you been? I thought you'd never get here."

"I couldn't get away; then I had to go home to get this wig before I went down town after the trailer." The newcomer's hand went to his thick, dark hair. "Why'd my mother have to give me red hair? Everybody sees it a mile away and knows me."

Now Jennie knew the driver of the truck. It was Pete Campbell! No wonder she hadn't recognized him with his red hair hidden under a wig. Well, if he had to disguise himself, and Gordon had to dye Fair Lady's white socks, these two were up to no good. And Pete had tried to make the state trooper suspicious of Dan Gray Wolf, recalled Jennie. What a nerve! Why, Pete must have been the one who put the saddle pad in Dan's car!

She still couldn't understand why Gordon would steal his own filly. Maybe Fair Lady wasn't his horse? Cramped and uncomfortable though she was, crouched behind the bush, Jennie made up her mind to stay until she had more pieces of the puzzle.

The moon came out from behind the cloud, illuminating the scene more brightly.

"Where are the papers?" asked Pete.

Trent reached into his jacket pocket and pulled out an envelope which he handed to Pete. "Here they are. You're selling a fine, rare, all-black Arabian."

Pete looked up sharply. "Yeah? What about her socks?"

"Look at them." Trent sounded proud of himself.

"Well, I'll be! How long will it take for that stuff to wash off?"

"It won't wash off! It'll grow out in time. But by then she'll be miles away and no one will be able to find you—or me."

"They won't find you," grumbled Pete. "I take all the chances while you stay out of sight and get most of the money."

"Oh, come on! You're making more in two nights than Harvey pays you in a month."

Pete was not convinced. "You get the lion's share of the price for the horses, plus the insurance money for Fair Lady." He came closer to Trent. "If you ask me, you're stupid to get rid of that filly. You don't need the money. Your pa left you plenty besides Fair Lady. What makes you so greedy?"

"Shut up!" snapped Trent. "We don't have time to fight about it. Let's get this horse in the trailer and on the road."

Pete said nothing but he opened the rear doors of the

trailer and let down the ramp. "I hope we don't have no trouble with her like we did with Venus. I couldn't get another shot. Harvey has the medicine locked up."

So they had given Venus an injection of something to quiet her down. That's why the whinny had stopped all at once. Probably they had given her a shot of some kind of tranquilizer. Jennie had seen that done on TV when people were capturing wild animals.

A small swarm of mosquitoes had raised welts on her neck and face but now, more than ever, she realized she must remain quiet.

Pete seized Fair Lady's bridle and led her to the trailer. She went easily enough until she put one foot on the ramp. Then she shied away. Pete brought her around again but she reared up and refused to obey.

He reached over and picked up a stick from the ground but before he had a chance to use it Trent stopped him. "You *will* have trouble if you whip her. She's scared now."

"She's your horse, you go ahead and load her," said Pete. He threw down the switch and walked away.

Trent stared after him. "Some stable boy you are! Can't even handle a horse. Where's that hood?" He walked Fair Lady across the clearing as if to calm her.

Pete went to the cab of the truck and returned with something white that looked like a bag. He thrust it into Trent's hands.

Trent was still grumbling at Pete. "You don't have

the nerve to make a good horse thief. You're so chicken you couldn't even be a chicken thief!"

This seemed to make Pete furious. He whirled around and faced Trent with his head thrust forward like a snake ready to strike. "You should talk about being chicken! You even have to hide behind your kid sister!"

This apparently hit Gordon in a tender spot. He twisted the white hood in his hand and snarled, "I don't hide behind anybody! All Miranda did was keep Bill Tomilsin busy so he wouldn't come home at the wrong time."

Jennie heard this with amazement. Miranda! What did she have to do with Gordon Trent? Then suddenly she understood. Gordon Trent must be Miranda's stepbrother, the one she rarely saw any more. Miranda had called him Gary, so Gordon Trent must be an assumed name. What power did he have over her that he could get her to help him steal the horses? Was she willing to help him because he had been so kind to her when her mother and stepfather had been killed?

Pete was still arguing with Gordon—or Gary. Jennie still couldn't think of him as anything but Gordon Trent. "You talk too much," said Pete. "Why'd you have to tell her everything you're going to do? Do you know she came over to see me at the stables the night we made off with Venus? She tried to talk me out of it. Said poor Venus had a colt and we shouldn't separate them! She was crying and carrying on. What if Harvey'd heard her?"

So that was where Miranda had been the night she had come running down the road with her slacks muddy and torn, thought Jennie. Yes, that was the night Venus had been stolen, the night when they had heard her wild whinny.

Pete was still complaining. "We'd of finished this job last night if you hadn't let Miranda and those other kids catch you in the barn."

"It's safer tonight," said Trent. "Everyone's at the picnic."

"By the way," said Pete. "I want some of that saddle money. No sense your stealing that saddle last night."

Oh, I was wrong, thought Jennie. Gordon stole the saddle, so he must have been the one who left the saddle pad in Dan's car.

"If you hadn't been so slow about bringing me the money for Venus I wouldn't have had to pawn the saddle," grumbled Trent. "So forget it."

"How come you need money so bad?" Pete's tone was insolent.

Trent's patience seemed to snap and he seized Pete by the front of his shirt. "I've heard enough out of you!"

Pete yanked himself free. Jennie could hear the shirt tear as he did so. "The sooner I'm through with you, the better, big shot!"

With a shrug Trent turned again to Fair Lady, and as he did so his entire manner changed. "Now, girl," he said gently, "we're going to take you for a little ride and nobody's going to hurt you. We'll just cover up your head so you won't be scared. It'll be just like going to a horse show. Here we go."

Trent deftly slipped the white bag over the filly's head, and then taking the bridle and talking quietly to her all the way, he led her toward the trailer.

He was speaking softly, for Fair Lady's ears alone, but as he came close to the trailer Jennie could hear him.

"You know I wouldn't part with you if there was any other way," he was saying. "Easy, girl! Too bad those horses over at Fort Erie aren't as good to me as you are. Let's face it. My luck's rotten."

Pete Campbell, still on the far side of the clearing, obviously could not hear Trent's remarks.

Still talking, Gordon led Fair Lady up the ramp and into the trailer. After that Jennie couldn't hear him or see what he was doing. She guessed that he was removing the hood from Fair Lady's head and fastening a strap to hold her steady in the trailer. He came back and closed the doors of the carrier.

Even though Trent wasn't as good a rider as Bill, he knew how to handle horses, thought Jennie. At least he could manage Fair Lady, but perhaps that was because he loved her.

Horses must be Trent's whole life, she surmised. He had mentioned Fort Erie. There was a race track there. Had he bet on the races and lost? Was he stealing Venus and Fair Lady to make up for his losses at the track? He must be desperate to do that.

As Trent left the trailer, Pete greeted him with a

sarcastic, "Very good. How come you're selling that horse when you're so crazy about her?"

Trent did not answer this. He said only, "When will you be back? Sunday night?"

"I'd better be. I have to be at work Monday morning or Harvey might get suspicious. In fact, I think he is, anyway."

"Call me as soon as you get back," Trent said. "I want that money no later than Monday night."

"You'll get it when I'm good and ready," Pete said sulkily.

"You come through with it or I'll drop the word that I saw you hanging around Fair Lady," Gordon threatened.

Pete came close to Trent and looked defiantly into his face. "You do that and you'll never collect the insurance for that horse."

With that he turned on his heel and strode to the truck. A moment later he drove off down the lane.

CHAPTER
16

Now that Pete Campbell had left with Fair Lady, Jennie expected that Gordon Trent would get into his car at once and leave. Instead, he lighted a cigarette and paced up and down, smoking.

Jennie was impatient for him to go. As long as he stayed, she was afraid to move. The woods and fields were silent and if she stirred he would surely hear her. As the minutes passed she became more and more aware of the danger she was in. Gordon couldn't afford to have anyone know that he was connected with the disappearance of the two horses. He would be furious if he found out she had heard him talking with Pete Campbell.

What kind of man was he? she wondered. Miranda was fond of him and Jennie knew that he was kind to Fair Lady. As a matter of fact, he had always been pleasant to Bill and to her. But, she realized, there were dark, hidden byways in his character.

By now Pete Campbell and Fair Lady would be on the

Blacknose Spring Road, heading for Buffalo or Rochester or other points beyond. Jennie knew she had to get back to Cloud quickly and ride to the nearest phone to call the police, or perhaps Uncle Fred was home by now and she could call from his house.

Trent showed no signs of leaving. He had sat down on a tree stump near the center of the clearing and he remained there with his head in his hands, motionless except when he placed his cigarette in his mouth. As soon as he finished one cigarette he lighted another from the butt. Jennie guessed that he wanted to be sure Pete and Fair Lady were well on their way before he left. He wouldn't want to take a chance of being seen near them.

How had he gotten both the car and horse here, anyway? He must have driven the car down the lane, then walked back to the barn for Fair Lady. He probably rode her through the fields and woods to avoid being seen.

With every minute she waited, Jennie knew Fair Lady was farther away. She decided that she must take a chance. If she could get in touch with the troopers before Gordon left, they might be able to capture him here.

Cautiously she crawled backward, keeping her eyes on the figure in the clearing. A branch of coralberry bush beside her shifted as she brushed against it, and Gordon's head turned toward the sound.

Jennie froze. Slowly Trent got to his feet and flung aside his cigarette.

"Who's there?" he demanded.

Jennie did not move. Deliberately the man walked toward her.

He stopped at the edge of the clearing. "I know you're in there," he said in a cold voice that sent a chill up Jennie's back. "You might as well come out."

With her heart pounding, Jennie waited, hoping he would decide he was mistaken.

Then, like a pouncing cat, Gordon Trent sprang toward her. He crashed through the bush that had sheltered her and landed on his feet only an arm's length away.

Jennie leaped back and eluded his reaching hands by inches. Whirling around, she fled blindly. It didn't matter where she went as long as she could stay ahead of Gordon.

Neither one of them spoke but before long Jennie could hear her own rasping breath as she began to tire. She knew she could not go much farther. It was difficult to run on the uneven ground. Her toe caught in the root of a tree and she almost fell.

Trent was closer now. He gasped, "Wait, Jennie!"

So he, too, was out of breath. If she could last a little longer she might be able to escape him. In a burst of speed, she left the cover of the woods, crossed a small clearing, and found herself among the cherry trees. She slackened her pace to draw a deep breath and listen. Heavy steps pounded behind her and spurred her to new effort. Here, though the ground was more open, the low-hanging branches were a hazard. Ripe cherries pelted to the ground as she ran. Mentally she apologized to the farmer who owned the orchard. I can't help it, she thought. I'll pick all day free to pay him back, if I ever get out of this.

Not far ahead and to the right Cloud was waiting behind Uncle Fred's house. Jennie tried to steer in that direction. Her chest ached so badly she was sure her heart was thudding against her ribs. Her vision blurred, making it difficult to distinguish the trees from the shadows. In her confusion, the patches of moonlight on the ground between the rows of trees looked like snow.

At last, exhausted, she blundered into a tree trunk and, with her arms around it, sank to the ground, drawing short, gasping breaths like a fish out of water.

He'll catch me now, she thought dully, but I can't go another step. She sat helplessly on the ground waiting for Trent to come.

It took several moments for her to realize that the footsteps behind her had stopped. She raised her head and found that she could see clearly again, though she could find nothing within her view but the trunks of the cherry trees, each rising from its own mound of dirt. Gordon was no place to be seen.

She couldn't believe her good fortune. Still breathing heavily, she pulled herself to her feet. Trent must have had to give up before she did. His legs were longer than hers so he should have been able to catch her long ago, she thought. But he did smoke all the time. That would make him get winded. If she hurried she might be able to get out of here, after all.

If only she knew which way to go! In her terror she had lost track of direction. Realizing she must be careful lest she walk back toward Gordon, she looked anxiously up and down the rows of trees.

To her left she saw a wide strip of moonlight. That must be the lane! Even though she would be less sheltered there, it might be better for her to follow it as she could be sure of her direction.

She left the comforting shadow of the tree trunk and hurried between the rows of cherry trees toward the ribbon of moonlight. When she reached the lane, she looked cautiously to the left and right and stared intently at the woods that bordered the opposite side of the road.

Reassured by the emptiness of the lane and the silence, she turned right and ran as fast as her aching chest would let her and then slowed to a walk only long enough to catch her breath. Every now and then she looked back over her shoulder to see if Gordon were following her.

As she rounded a familiar bend in the lane she realized that she had traveled in a circle as she fled from Trent, for she was farther from Blacknose Spring Road than she had believed. This spurred her to an even greater effort.

She thought longingly of a warm bath and bed, but first she must call the police and then tell Bill about Fair Lady.

Of course he and Miranda might not be home yet. After listening to Pete Campbell and Trent in the clearing, Jennie knew why Miranda had clung to Bill all day. She had wanted to make sure that he did not go home and surprise Gordon making off with Fair Lady. This knowledge erased much of the bitterness of the hours spent at the picnic. Thinking back, she realized that Miranda had not enjoyed the day, either. Running from one thing to another and exclaiming over everything had been an act.

Gordon, too, had put on a big act, pretending he was worried that someone would steal Fair Lady. Buying the padlock was a part of the game, just as he had taken the door from its hinges because that way no one would suspect him for a minute. He had known people would think that a man with a key would not go to all that trouble.

Deep in thought, Jennie did not see the tall shadow move out of the woods into the lane ahead of her. When she looked up and saw Gordon Trent it was too late. His lean face, white in the moonlight, filled her with terror.

CHAPTER
17

With a gasp of fright Jennie stepped back to run, but in two strides Trent caught her arm in a merciless grip. In his left hand she saw a long white handkerchief or cloth of some kind which he raised toward her face.

Jennie drew a deep breath and screamed. Instantly Gordon clamped his hand over her mouth with rough force and threw her to the ground. Her head hit the lane with a jarring thwack. Although she fought with all her strength he was larger and stronger than she and within five minutes she lay gagged and bound hand and foot with strips from Gordon's shirt.

Exhausted from her struggle, she lay watching the man who stood above her, breathing heavily. Her arms ached from their awkward position and the stones of the lane bit into her back.

Trent walked away and then returned. He looked down at her, opened his mouth as if about to speak, and then strode away again.

Jennie hoped he would not come back, but a moment later he towered beside her, asking in an annoyed voice, "What am I going to do with you?"

Jennie wished she could say, "Just leave me here," but the gag made words impossible.

Gordon ran his hand nervously through his hair, leaving it rumpled. "No use asking you not to tell. You'd go to the police first thing." His voice became angrier. "You stupid girl! Last thing I want is a murder rap!"

Fear stabbed at Jennie's breast and she rolled her head from side to side, fixing Trent with pleading eyes.

If only the police would come! She had lost track of time, but she was sure more than an hour had passed since she had called them. Perhaps they had been here already and gone. They might have come when she and Gordon were far up the lane. After all, she had told them the truck would be in the clearing near the entrance to the lane. They wouldn't expect it to be almost to Kienuka.

Trent's eyes darted toward the macadam road and the lake beyond. "That's the place for you," he muttered, glancing down at Jennie.

She stared at him, horror-stricken. Was he planning to throw her into the lake?

"You brought this on yourself," Trent said, his tone more menacing than before. "Look, you young Indian, I'm not going to spend the best part of my life in jail just because of one snoopy girl!"

Trent paused to light a cigarette. When he spoke again he was quieter but no less threatening.

"I'll let you in on a secret," he whispered, "because you aren't going to be around to squeal on me."

He leaned over Jennie and blew a cloud of smoke into her face. "I borrowed a little money from the insurance company where I work—just a few thousand—and I lost it all on the races."

Trent straightened. "My boss is getting wise to me. He's ordered a special audit of my books next week, so I have to put the money back before then or I'll land in jail and my chances of getting another good job will be finished for life."

Jennie lay breathlessly still. He wouldn't be telling her this if he had any idea of letting her live.

Gordon was still talking, as much to himself as to her. "Venus helped. If I get enough for Fair Lady I might make it yet." He gave a nervous laugh. "Justice, isn't it? I lose everything on the horses. And horses help me get it back." He glared at Jennie. "And then *you* came along!"

Jennie saw the glowing cigarette butt arc through the air as Gordon tossed it away. Again her captor disappeared. This time she could hear him hurrying down the lane toward Blacknose Spring Road. Jennie guessed that he was making sure the way was clear.

So he had been stealing money from the company for which he worked. She wondered how he did that. Perhaps some people paid their premiums in cash or made out their checks to the agent's name.

It was hard to understand why Miranda liked Gordon so much. He must have changed a lot since he had gotten into trouble. Or was it just that Miranda didn't really know what he was like?

At any rate, he had gotten himself into a corner now, and he sounded as if he were desperate.

Jennie realized this might be her last hour of life. Bound like this she surely would drown if he tossed her into the lake. The stars had never looked so beautiful.

Tears came into her eyes and ran down the sides of her face. The mingled scent of cherries and fresh earth was perfume, and in that moment she knew how much she loved the reservation and the people in it. How had she ever doubted for a minute that this was where she belonged? She was an Indian and she wanted to do everything she could to help her people. If she could study music she would come back here and teach the Tuscarora children. Grandma and Grandpa—and Bill— would feel terrible if Gordon killed her.

He wasn't going to kill her! She wouldn't let him! Jennie snapped out of her self-pity and put her mind onto ways of escape. Time. Time was on her side. If she could just hold off long enough Bill would come home and notice that Fair Lady was missing. Or the troopers might come.

If only she could hide from Gordon! Jennie arched her back and pushed with her heels. Yes, bound though she was, she could still roll. By the time Gordon returned, she had hidden in the brush north of the road. She heard his angry exclamation when he discovered she wasn't where he had left her, but to her sorrow he quickly located her.

Seizing her roughly under the arms, he pulled her down the lane. Jennie dragged her heels and clutched at rocks in the road with her bound hands. Blacknose Spring Road—and the lake—were not far away.

Gordon was breathing hard and soon he stopped to rest. As she lay there, Jennie heard someone call her name. Gordon apparently heard it, too, for he raised his head and stiffened.

"Jen-nie!"

It was Bill Tomilsin's voice. Jennie pushed frantically at the gag with her tongue. If only she could call back to him!

Running footsteps sounded on the lane and the beam of a flashlight briefly touched the leaves overhead.

Gordon reacted swiftly. Within seconds he had her off the track and hidden in the bushes. There he crouched over her, holding her down.

Jennie heard her uncle shout, "Bill! Cloud's behind the house!" What was Uncle Fred doing here? she wondered. A moment later she heard him a little nearer, saying, "I found Jennie's hair ribbon on the ground. What d'you make of that?"

She heard Miranda sob, "Something's happened to Jennie! I know it!" she sounded hysterical.

Bill's voice was tense. "What happened? Out with it, Miranda!"

"Gary took Fair Lady," she burst out. "He said he'd kill anyone who tried to stop him! We have to find him —quick!"

"Who's Gary?" demanded Bill.

"Gordon Trent. Gary's his real name. He's my stepbrother. Someone was going to meet him down the lane with a trailer."

Jennie could feel the tenseness of her captor's muscles. Miranda was still sobbing. "Don't let him know I told on him," she begged.

"Come on." It was Dan Gray Wolf's voice. "Let's follow these tire tracks. We may not be too late!"

Jennie squirmed desperately and Gordon moved his hand to her throat. His palm pressed against her windpipe.

It was now or never, thought Jennie. When the searchers were out of sight Gordon would surely act. With a strength she had not guessed she possessed, she raised her knees against her chest and kicked straight up into Trent's stomach. She caught him off balance and with a gasp he toppled sideways. In that instant she rolled and hunched her way back to the lane. Gordon came crashing after her but he was too late. Bill was racing toward her.

Trent leaped past them and ran down the lane toward the road.

Miranda screamed, "Gary!" and tried to stop him. He

pushed her aside and kept running, but, before he had gone far, powerful headlights flashed on at the end of the lane. The revolving light of a police car sent red flames quivering among the trees.

Trent plunged to the right toward the cherry orchard but Dan Gray Wolf seized him. A trooper jumped from the patrol car and helped Dan pull Gordon to the car.

In the meantime Bill had removed the gag from Jennie's mouth and had untied her hands and feet. Gently he helped her to stand.

It felt good to lean on him. "I'm so glad you're here," she said gratefully. "How'd you ever find me?"

Bill pulled her closer and for a second she felt his cheek against her head. "It was partly because of Dan. He went to my house looking for me because it was late and he thought the picnic would be over. When he noticed the barn door was broken open and Cloud and Fair Lady were gone, he came to the picnic grounds to see if by any chance I was still there. Of course he found Miranda and me. Then we picked up your Uncle Fred outside your house."

"He was supposed to be at the party!"

"I know," said Bill. He put his arm around her and they started slowly down the lane. "He said you wouldn't back out of your cousin's party without a good reason, so he went to the house to be sure you weren't sick. When we couldn't find you there I was sure you must've headed for the lane. You came here on Cloud, didn't you?"

Jennie nodded. "The troopers were on an accident call and couldn't come right away so I just thought I'd find out where Fair Lady was . . ."

Bill gave her a gentle shake. "You could've gotten killed."

Jennie agreed. "Gordon—Gary—was going to drown me. He needs money—and he'll do anything to get it. He and Pete Campbell stole Venus and Fair Lady, too. Gary was going to sell Fair Lady and collect on her insurance. He'd pretend someone else had stolen her."

"That Miranda!" Bill's voice was hoarse with anger. "She never gave me a clue till a minute ago when it was almost too late to save you. And I stuck with her all day, hoping I'd get the truth out of her."

"She did tell you, though, when she knew I was in danger," Jennie reminded him.

Bill stopped and put both hands on her shoulders. He looked deep into her eyes. "Don't you *ever* go off alone like this again!"

"Don't worry, I won't!"

They were nearing the end of the lane. Miranda ran toward them and flung her arms around Jennie. Jennie held her close. Miranda was just awfully mixed up, she thought. And she'd been trying to protect her stepbrother. After this was all over maybe she'd be like her old self.

As soon as the troopers had Jennie's description of Pete Campbell and the trailer they drove away with

Gordon Trent. Then Bill led Jennie to Dan Gray Wolf's car which was parked beside the road.

"Cloud—" began Jennie.

"I'll ride him home," offered Dan. He tossed his keys to Bill.

"I saved supper for you," Jennie said reproachfully.

"I'm sorry," apologized Dan. "I fell asleep after work and didn't wake up till dark."

Grandma and Grandpa were home when they arrived and everyone gathered in the kitchen.

After Jennie had recounted her night's experiences, Grandma turned to Miranda. "Now, young lady, what have you to say for yourself?"

Miranda lifted her chin defiantly. "I tried to stop Gary as soon as I knew he was going to take Venus, but he wouldn't pay any attention to me."

"You should have told me," said Grandma, "or the police."

Tears began to run down Miranda's already tear-stained face. "I didn't want Gary to go to jail. I never thought he'd hurt Jennie. I didn't know he was so—wild."

"You never let on he was your stepbrother," said Bill. "How come?"

"When he first came here he told me it was going to be our secret—you know, that we were related. I thought it was fun, like a game. I didn't know why he wanted it that way." Miranda mopped her eyes with a wet tissue. "He was so kind to me after my mother died —so different. He scares me the way he is now."

"I'm sure Gary is scared, too." Uncle Fred put his hand on Jennie's shoulder. "The way he treated Jennie showed how scared he was . . ."

"Fear does strange things to people," said Grandma. "A strong man can face it and come out stronger, but a weak one will do almost anything to save his own neck."

"What'll happen to Gary now?" Miranda asked.

"He'll spend some time in prison, that's certain," answered Uncle Fred. "After that? It depends on how much he wants to change."

"That ghost horse,' said Jennie suddenly. "What was that all about?"

"Yes," put in Grandma. "Please."

Miranda turned appealing eyes to Jennie. "Gary told me about the skeleton horse a long time ago. Some Indian friend of his told him about it. Then that night when I heard Venus making all that noise, I just said I saw a ghost horse so you wouldn't realize a real horse was being stolen."

"You made things worse for yourself and Gary," said Bill. "That story made us curious."

Grandma looked shocked. "And to think I believed you!" As if she were too upset to remain still, she jumped up and went to the refrigerator for a pitcher of lemonade.

Miranda said helplessly, "I didn't dare tell you the truth for fear you'd suspect me."

Grandma shook her head sadly. "Miranda, you have a few things to learn."

"I learned a lot this week," replied Miranda. "It was awful."

The phone rang in the living room and Uncle Fred answered it. He returned with good news. "The police found Fair Lady and Pete Campbell a mile this side of Lockport," he announced. "They've arrested Pete and he has told them where to find Venus."

"Oh, good!" cried Miranda. "Now the colt will have his mother back."

Everyone laughed, and the tension eased. Grandma set out a plate of cookies and Miranda helped her pour the lemonade.

"Jennie," said Uncle Fred. "Did you wonder where I was the night Venus was stolen?"

She nodded mutely.

"I was at your guidance teacher's. We had an appointment to talk about your music and the possibility of college. We have it all worked out now if you want to go. You'll get the Indian assistance money from the state, of course, and maybe you can get a scholarship. Your father will help, too. I didn't want to say anything until we knew it was possible."

Jennie smiled gratefully at him and then asked hesitantly, "Grandma, what do you say?"

Grandma answered in her usual pert way, "How can I stop a girl who isn't even afraid to go chasing after a ghost horse?"

"But there wasn't any ghost horse!" protested Jennie.

"Maybe yes and maybe no." Grandma's bright eyes took in the weary group around the kitchen. "Aren't we all safe tonight in spite of the danger we were in? I say the spirits are still watching over us Indians."

Jennie met Bill's eyes and he gave her an understanding smile that said more than an embrace.

ABOUT THE AUTHOR

Margaret Goff Clark lives just outside the city of Niagara Falls, near the Tuscarora Indian Reservation. At her adoption by the Senecas in July, 1962, she was given the Indian name of Deh-yi-sto-esh, meaning She Who Writes and Publishes.

Writing has been a lifetime interest, for she started composing verse at the age of seven. Her more than two hundred short stories, many one-act plays, and poems have appeared in young peoples' magazines, reading books, and anthologies.

A graduate of the State University College at Buffalo, New York, she taught in the elementary grades and junior high school for six years.

Besides *Mystery Horse,* the author has written nine other books, most of them mysteries. "I like to read suspense stories," she says, "so I guess it's natural that I like to write them."

Mrs. Clark's interests, which include swimming, travel, mountain climbing, history, and archeology, often find their way into her writing.

The author is married to Charles R. Clark, a former classmate in college. They are the parents of two children, Robert, a radiologist in San Francisco, and Marcia, a nurse in Los Angeles.